THE ONE-WAY RAIN

THE ONE-WAY RAIN

Cathy Jacobowitz

To Jessica
my dear love.
Cathy
8/17/2013

Wildheart Press
Boston, MA
2013

This is a work of fiction. Any resemblance to actual
persons, living or dead, is entirely coincidental.

Designed by Eben Sorkin

ISBN 978-0-9663097-0-6

Wildheart Press
P.O. Box 230658
Boston MA 02123

ABOUT THE COVER:
Devynity is a writer and performer from South Jamaica,
Queens, whose words tell the stories that have yet to be heard.
Get into her music at www.devynity.com. Photograph of
Devynity © and courtesy Johnette Marie Ellis. Photograph of
roses © Kyle Katz. Cover designed by Steve Wolf.

To my person, Kyle Katz.

By 1999, with its acquisition of Lollybella Fundustries, Sirocco's hold on power was complete. It controlled not only the economy of the United States but its government as well. In accordance with the strategic plan developed by Clark and Davis in the seventies, the company's immense structure remained virtually invisible to the public eye, while its thousands of brands appeared to compete with each other in a vibrant free marketplace.

A crisis was brewing, however. Since the war began, Vesperian, Inc., had been methodically cutting off Sirocco's access to export processing zones in Southeast Asia. Without a stream of extremely low-cost, high-profit consumer goods, the company's financial model was threatened. It was young Phelps, the budget analyst out of Chicago, who suggested the scheme that would determine the course of American society for the next fifty years. Why not, he asked, create export processing zones right here at home? He laid it out for the executive team over drinks at a strip club: a catastrophic strike on a U.S. city, leading to widespread fear and panic. Followup strikes decimating certain areas. A legislative package creating special assistance districts, unfettered by labor regulation, where qualified individuals could be relocated and provided with manufacturing jobs. Additional legislation providing for adequate supervision of those districts.

"But who would those qualified individuals be?" asked Jan Courtney, VP for Human Resources. To which Phelps replied, "Who do you think?"

From *The Long Fall of Sirocco: African-American Resistance, 2001-2045*, by E. A. Hunt

Lady Hazel, slender dreadlocks twined with flowers, comes to announce it is market day. "Your Majesty," she says, "would that not be a lark, to go among the common people?"

"You must not mock the common people, Hazel," says the Queen. "They too are deserving of our love."

She gets up. It is spewing down rain, and the tarp is flapping in the wind, making a sound like a heavy fist pounding a wooden door. "My lady," Hazel says, "Sir Mordred is come to harangue you."

"I have nothing to say to that man," the Queen says.

Hazel says, "I shall tell him begone."

"Or we will have the Sergeant-at-Arms after him," the Queen says. Her new Sergeant-at-Arms is a loyal servant, despite his provoking dalliance with Ladies Angelica and Angelina, the twins.

Wrapped in trash bags, her appurtenances clanking, she goes out to check the bucket and finds less than an inch of water. What did she do wrong? She's always doing something wrong. Now she sees she didn't place it far enough away from the tarp. But you can't leave your bucket sitting out in the open. No matter how hidden and secluded you think your nest is, the moment you leave anything in the open somebody will come along and find it. Then they'll come and find you.

Her stomach is like an old wound that reopens every morning. She snaps at Lady Daffodil to bring her some cinnamon toast and a flask of chocolate. Now!

Inside her nest, hidden in a mound of dirt near the pitty wall, she has a jug of river water. She hoists the jug and allows a small amount of water to trickle into the bucket. When the level is just high enough to cover the hose-end of her water filter, she puts down the jug, pulls the filter out of her shirts, sticks the hose in the bucket (where it twists and flops out of the water like a dying snake) and starts pumping. After five minutes she lifts up the filter and carefully unscrews the little metal cup attached to its base. The cold orange-brown water smells metallic and tastes delicious. She saves a little to damp her fingers in, cleans crust from her eyes and rubs her teeth.

Now that the ladies have attended to her toilette, where the heck is Daffodil with breakfast? "I want her whipped," she says. "Whipped and stocked." That Daffodil is a lazy beast.

The cooking pot was not wiped clean after last night's banquet of cattail roots, so she sets Lady Susan to chip away at the hardened scum with a stick. Afterwards she pushes the pot under a jag of concrete and piles last year's rotten leaves in front of it. The kinked metal rod that supports the pot is still propped over the fire, so she takes it down and hides it in the leaves. She rakes apart the nearly extinguished embers. Her fear of fire is strong, but the nights are still too cold—she thinks it is March—to go without one. She bids the court farewell. Lady Hazel slides after her, like a ghost.

She doesn't go the most direct way, through The Lanes. Half the houses there have collapsed and the rest are full of crazy people. Instead she takes the long route, down the railroad tracks to the old elementary school, then across the ruined highway and around the cemetery to the baseball field. Because it is raining, and because polices can fly through the sky, the merchants are crowded into the bleachers under a corrugated roof. Sodden figures jostle her as they climb past.

She is wearing twice her weight in clothes, including a hooded parka and three bandanas tied around her head and neck, but the vendor knows she is a girl. "Take your time, angel," he says. "Have a look."

She points at a battered, half-empty tube of toothpaste. He wants to know what she's got. Reaching under her parka, she fishes out a short piece of ball chain.

"Bracelet," she says. He is unmoved. "No clasp, love," he says.

She tries some rusty nails. "Got a million of 'em," he says. She hesitates, reviewing the other items in her bag with her fingertips. Finally she brings out a watch battery. "Can't move those," the man says. "No demand."

She is turning away when he gives her the Crest. "Thank you," she says.

He is handsome, with long, well-kept braids and smooth skin. "Got a toothbrush to go with it?" he says.

She shakes her head. He beckons her with one finger, and she climbs over the seats to join him. Someone comes along wanting coffee. "I got your Postum," the man says. "Got your Sanka packets. Chicory too."

"I said coffee, brother, can't you hear?"

"Chicory and barley mix, it boil up real nice."

"Fuck you."

"No, brother, fuck you."

Rain thuds on the metal roof. He turns to her. "You on your own?" She shakes her head. "You got a name?"

"Reka," she says. He says, "Reka, my name Cesario." They shake hands: his is sheathed in supple leather. Now that she is close up to him she can tell he smells warm, like leather and embers. He keeps hold of her hand. "You just a little thing," he says. "How old are you, twelve?"

As this is exactly how old she is, she doesn't know how to respond. The Traveler told her never to reveal any personal information, but she doesn't like to lie. She gives a tiny nod.

"And where's your family, little thing?" She doesn't say anything. "Gone?"

"No," Reka says.

"Nothing to be ashamed of. We all in the same boat." He gives her hand a squeeze before he lets it go, and the squeeze feels nice. "I lost my mama in the second surge."

"My grandma," she says, before she can stop herself. Even though it happened far away from here, she worries that news of her guilt has spread. But he says nothing, only pats her on the shoulder. A woman wrapped in blankets walks up and shows them a spool of orange thread with a needle stuck into it. Cesario says no, then yes. He lets the woman pick out a matchbook marked El Toreador, and when she's gone he hands Reka the spool. "You know how to use that?" She nods, clutching it. It is a beautiful orange like a stuffed dog she had a long time ago. "Listen up," he says, "I know how you live."

This confuses her. How does he know where her nest is? She has never seen him before. He says, "Some hidey-hole under a bridge. When it rains, you get wet. If you eat a rat it's a good day. And ain't nobody coming around to tuck you in at night."

The wind pricks up tears in her eyes and one rolls down her face, stingingly cold. She flinches away from Cesario's hand, but he's just removing the teardrop: he shows it to her, a blacker spot on black leather, then rubs it away between two fingertips.

"You ain't seen your family in three, four years. Maybe they can't find you, maybe they don't want to. Or else they dead." He lifts another tear from her face. "Either way, you alone. Twelve year old and you look ten. What you gonna do next, Reka baby? Where you gonna go?"

"I have a place," she says.

"You start bleeding yet?"

Alarmed, she looks down at herself. All she sees is clothing, no flesh and certainly no blood. Cesario starts to laugh, pulls her in, gives her a sweet-smelling hug. She wants to fall asleep between his arm and his side. "I know a place you can stay, baby," he says.

"You do?"

"Pretty little house. In The Lanes. No bomb damage, no cracked windows. Central heat. Are you familiar with that concept—central heat?"

"How much?" she asks. She doesn't think a watch battery, three nails and a chewed-up pencil will get her a night in a place like that. Besides, she wants to keep the pencil in case she ever finds a piece of paper.

"Food too. Plenty of it. You eat every scrap on that table, they still plenty left over. More food than you know what to do with."

Cold air is seeping between the seams of her parka.

She doesn't remember being warm. Cold is a condition of existence, like hunger, like fear. "It don't cost nothing, to answer your question," the man says. "This house is my business premises."

Something's wrong. She wants to be there in that house with him—that's what's wrong.

"I gotta go," she says, wriggling out of his embrace. Suddenly his hand is around her elbow. "Think about it," Cesario says. "You just a kid. It's a miracle you ain't dead yet. How much longer you think you got?"

She tries to yank her arm free. "And what about next year?" he says. He opens his hand and she reels away, her feet scrabbling on icy cement. "What about when they smell that blood?" She is off and running, slamming into people as she hurtles down the steps. She hears Cesario call out, "I can't do nothing for you then."

Hazel joins her as she walks home. "I will have him stocked," she says, but Reka hardly hears her. The truth is, she has never been able to eat a rat. She feels too much akin to them. She could be one herself, a twitching, skittering, scampering rat, turning tail and hiding at the first sign of trouble. The Traveler would never have abandoned a human child, but everybody will abandon a rat.

I

MATERIALITY

Day 1

Sterling Teacher hated this life.

WHEN YOU'RE DOWN . . . WEAR BLUE
REVELATION!

She had hated it ever since she was a small child.

GINKGO TREE FARMACEUTICALS: YOUR
HEALTH.

She knew she was not like other people.

FREE TRIAL—INDIGO SEX LABS.

And she hated the people she wasn't like.

GOVERNEQUALITY NORTH HARBOR. GARBAGE
REMOVAL IS ON US.

The stream of popshow above, around and below them,
across walls, ceilings, sidewalks, trees, on glass, water, grass,
skin, on food and toilet paper—it didn't bother other people.
They liked it. Or maybe they could ignore it. Sterling did
not have that talent. She suffered from a morbid sensitiv-
ity to popshow, which in her lifetime had still been called
advertising, and everything about it: the flickering lights
and colors, the endlessly repeated images, its fatuous humor
and moronic sentiment and especially its sublime confidence in its own power to shape her behavior. She could
not stand being taken for granted.

FUNNY FACE GUM ... BETTER GET SUM.

If popshow had been a person she would have killed it long
ago. Instead, she reserved to her stubborn, fanatic, and ulti-
mately malignant self the study of its slow destruction.

DON'T YOU WANT YOUR FIZZY SAMM'S?

North Harbor was a small city on the Atlantic seaboard.
It was also the country's largest producer of popshow. There
were ten major popshow agencies in the downtown area,

and Sterling had been inside seven of them. In six, she had engineered enough damage to result in a significant loss of revenue.

LOLLYWORLD ON THE BAY. LOLLYWORLD ON THE BAY. LOLLYWORLD ON THE BAY.

The seventh had been last week, and she was still not over it.

MY SOUL IS NOT FOR SALE.

"That's a new one, huh?"

Three years of work down the fucking toilet. All because George Mack wanted his Lollynut.

FREEDOMCHANNEL IS EVERYTHING YOU WANT TO KNOW. DIRECT TO YOUR TAP-TAP. LATEST WAR AND WEATHER.

Why the fuck didn't he keep a box of Lollynuts at his desk? How could he just wander away from the security station? She had a good mind to get him fired.

"Sterling, hey." It was a man she worked with, named Cleveland. He pointed to an image floating across the elevator wall. "It's different, huh?"

MY SOUL IS NOT FOR SALE. She had seen it, of course. She saw more popshow in one day than the brain of Cleveland Eddy, student brand advisor at the University of North Harbor, could process in a lifetime.

"It's interesting, don't you think? Using a black girl. Interesting choice."

The child in the picture was indeed darker than most of the population of North Harbor. "I like it," Cleveland said. "What do you think it's for?"

"How old are you?" Sterling said.

He answered reflexively, "Thirty-nine."

"You're thirty-nine years old, and you don't know what that ad is for?"

"Tell me."

"It's for a product you can't live without."

Cleveland Eddy just looked at her. Then, maddeningly, he smiled.

She had surveilled the building every night for six months. She had hacked into the company's tapnet. She had decrypted digital signatures and cloned keycards. She had memorized fifteen floors' worth of security schematics. Not to mention the expense, which was considerable. All to be damn near busted by a semi-retired jerkoff in the employee kitchenette.

DELICIOUS! GOLDEN! LOLLYNUTS NOW WITH BLUEBERRIES!!—she wanted to throw something.

In the past, the euphoria of success had carried her through the necessary waiting period between jobs. Without that deep, even narcotic satisfaction, everything seemed to prick her hard: every screen, flat, jumbo, and hype between campus and her apartment caught her right between the eyes. Her mood was not improved when she opened her front door to find her ex-lover sitting on the couch.

"What are you doing here?"

"I broke in," said Aimee, looking pleased with herself.

"Well, break out again."

"Don't you want to know how I did it?"

"No," Sterling said. Anyone could pick a tumbler lock.

"A client of Jamie's taught me."

"A real criminal? That must have been exciting for you." She put her bag down. "What do you want?"

"I worry about you, you know," Aimee said. She was a plump blondish person in a Sylvia Sugar blouse and skirt. Her stockings were embroidered with Ls for Lollybella and her shoes were by Great Adventure, also a Lolly company. "I like to make sure you're okay."

"Just say what you came for."

"Okay, you know that new flat?"

"Which fucking flat, Aimee?"

"The one that says 'My soul is not for sale.' "

Sterling was disgusted. "It's for jeans."

"No, I—" She paused. "Really?"

"What did you think it was for? Liberty and justice for all?"

Aimee frowned. She and her boyfriend were professional reformers, supposed activists who cycled through various nonprofit organizations. Both belonged to a "resistance" group called Independent United, which Aimee had founded in college and which, in Sterling's opinion, did absolutely nothing. "I didn't think that," she said.

"It's an ad for jeans, it was produced by Coyson Stone, it looks like stage one of a five- or six-week roll-out with a reveal at the end. Probably a Lolly brand packaged as something indie. What possible difference could it make?"

"Do you know who the model is?"

"Do you think I spend my time reading popshow magazines? I don't know who the model is."

"Can you find out?"

"What is this about?"

"You can't tell *anyone*, okay?" Aimee said. "Not a single freaking soul."

They had been contacted by the insurgents. They, Independent United, had received a letter, an actual letter, on paper, from inside SAPID, and they had agreed to host a leader of the rebellion, and that person was now here. In Aimee's apartment. Asking about the flat.

"Why?"

"I guess the kid looks familiar? Like she might be from SAPID too."

It did not strike Sterling as incredible that someone with the right tools, sufficient knowledge and a pair of brass balls could pull off an escape from SAPID. What she found completely unbelievable was that such a person would then waste two seconds on Aimee's klatsch of pocket Marxists.

"How did I.U. qualify for a rebel exchange program?" she said. "What are you going to teach this guy, how to make cute little posters and stick them up with wheatpaste?"

After Aimee left, thwarted and offended, Sterling could not sleep. Her bed seemed to become the rock-hard epicenter of failure, and George Mack's astonished countenance haunted the air. In the middle of the night she got up and looked out the window. She lived in an apartment tower surrounded by jumbos. From these billboards, a dozen of which were visible from her window, the same black head stared back at her: a young girl, eyes deep in shadow, her high forehead fading into the obscenity of the slogan.

Sterling usually did not look directly at popshow. She

didn't have to; she absorbed every detail of every picture the way salt drinks moisture. But now, gazing from her window, exhausted by vexation and a kind of irrational grief, she felt for a brief and peculiar moment that she was looking into the face of her own destruction.

Days 4-10

Above her desk the girl stared from a different angle, in front of a charred background of tree stumps and ruins. The words MY SOUL IS NOT FOR SALE shimmied across the wall. Sterling was beginning to conceive a real, specific hatred for this ad. It burned.

"What do you think it's for?"

"You asked me that last week."

"Oh, so I did," said Cleveland Eddy. "And you basically told me I was a moron."

He rested his forearms on the counter, dangling both hands into her office. The half of him that Sterling could see was clothed in a double-breasted suit jacket by Flight Plan for Arena, a UNoMe? Uomo silk tie tacked with an L-shaped pin, and gold earrings from Sapsucker. His watch, by Rumors of War, played tiny hypes for the new Paddy Duck longshow. "Can I help you with something?" she said.

"Yes, I have a check request that needs processing? For sixteen thousand dollars for Lollysnax?"

"You can submit that at the front office."

"I'm kidding, Sterling. Can I come in?"

He made himself at home in the extra chair, plucking at his pants before crossing one leg over the other and regarding her with open friendliness. He was deeply tanned, with freckles on his cheeks and a penumbra of amber-colored curls. "You know, Sterling, you're not like other girls."

"That's right. I'm gay."

He waved that off. "I mean you're an iconoclast. How long have you been working here?"

"Nine years."

"And in that time, have you ever decorated this office?

Have you ever put up one piece of popshow, or even put a poprock player in?"

"I don't listen to music."

"I like you, Sterling. Did you know that?"

"I'm becoming aware of it."

"I think you should have lunch with me."

"Excuse me?"

"Lunch!" he said, beaming. "Want to go over to the QuickGood? Step out to Lollyburger? We could see the new Smartinis hype in the library."

"I'm not interested."

"Come on, Sterling Teacher, it's on me."

"I would appreciate you leaving me alone to do my work."

"Ah, Sterling," he said fondly, seeming not at all disappointed. "Someday you'll change your mind."

Irritatingly, it was a good ad. Something about that face (looming in yet another iteration over the train station) caught even the jaded local eye; people in other parts of the country would eat it up. The agency style was as clear as a signature. Coyson Stone, the grand old house on Sassafras Street—she had destroyed their tapnet servers three years ago. The building had an atrium, ten stories high, surrounded by open floors and featuring an artificial rock wall. It was simply a question of scaling the wall, then swinging yourself over the balconies onto any floor you chose. She wished she had burned the place to the ground.

Policemen were checking bags in the neon-yellow glow of a Paddy Duck hype (PADDY PADS AGAIN! BROUGHT TO YOU BY RUMORS OF WAR). She queued, opened her knapsack, moved on. She was stopped again by a soldier in GovernEquality fatigues. "Miss, step over here please."

He scanned her with a tapwand, front and back. "Where's your chip?"

"I don't have one."

"I can't let you on the train."

"Here." She produced her crumpled passbook. He seemed reluctant to touch it. "Go on, tap me up. I'm in there."

The soldier went away. Sterling rested her head against

tiles imprinted with a variety of Lollysnax. She wondered if Coyson had really found their model on the other side of the wall. A kid off the street, maybe, without representation to drive up the price? Improbable, but not impossible. And Skip Stone was tight with the military authorities.

"You shouldn't be carrying paper around. It could lead to identity theft."

Let me handle that, she almost said, but stopped herself in time. She was flinging out bitterness and frustration like a centrifuge.

At home was no intruder, only silence and an empty refrigerator. She sat in the middle of the floor. Say they got their face in SAPID. Had they done the shoot there, or brought her here? The latter, she thought. The campaign was ongoing, and they'd want the model accessible but under wraps. What if she was still inside Coyson Stone?

Oh, this was not a good idea. You never went back to the site of a hit. Everything could have changed in three years: security cameras, motion detectors, perimeter sensors could all be in different places. One or more of the passageways she had used could be sealed off. Someone could be working late. The very objective was ridiculous: what would she do with the girl if she found her? Set her loose? Take her to Aimee's? Why not? Let Aimee and her little rebel band deal with it. Coyson was a big company, slow to change. She knew they had never remodeled the atrium, even though it was an obvious security risk. Three nights of surveillance would do it—say four. She had a good idea where the child might be, if they really had her. If not, away through the night and no harm done; but maybe the weight would drain from her arms and her legs, and the whirling in her head would stop.

"Moonface Burger? JuJuPie? Choco-lace Dreamdrink?"
"Salad," she said to the cook.
"Want some tea? They have Secret Pasha."
"Please stop offering me food," Sterling said.
"Chickaree Caesar, or Wild Spinach Fantasy?" said the

cook.

"The latter."

"Sorry?"

"She wants the Wild Spinach Fantasy," Cleveland said. "And can we have Crave-Me CranBits on that?"

He insisted on paying, proudly holding his thumb under the scanner as she returned the cash to her pocket. He found them a table by the window. "I love to people-watch, don't you?"

Dispiritedly she forked through her salad. Each Cran-Bit was emblazoned with a C and a trademark sign. It was her bad luck, she learned, that he was from Iowa, a place where people were naturally friendly. "Everyone here is so serious," he confided. "People never smile. For instance, you."

"Cleveland, there have got to be more interesting things in your life than me."

"Oh, there are!" Draping an arm over the back of his chair, he grinned at her. He had a wide grin that made him look like a piece of popshow. His vest was Forever Emerald, his shirt Compared To What. "But not right now. Not at one-fifteen in the afternoon on a Wednesday."

She had been awake for thirty hours. "I'm sorry," she said. "It must be hard to be so easily bored."

"Well, you know, I've tried it all," Cleveland said. "Drugs, drinking, sex. It just seems like the healthiest thing to do is be interested in other people."

They had made some superficial improvements, like scanning employees at the door and updating all alarm codes. But they had not changed the fundamental way the organization worked—its extreme top-down nature, which reposed most knowledge in Skip Stone and his deputies and left nine-tenths of the company just following orders. She knew Skip Stone well, though he did not know her. She knew he had instituted a master key system, apparently believing that a hacker would be stymied by a series of physical locks. Unfortunately for him, Sterling was not a hacker. She had jostled a vice-president early this morning, picked up his keys and handed them back to him. Then she went home and cut a master from memory, using a key blank and a file. The alarm codes she had ascertained through binoculars as the building was being shut down for the night.

"So. Tell me about yourself."

"I work in the reimbursement department."

"And I'm the student brand advisor. Come on, Sterling, throw me a bone."

She pushed her salad away. "Then will you let me go?"

"Yes," said Cleveland, "if you give me one tiny piece of information about yourself, you can call a halt to this lovely meal we are enjoying together."

"I don't like cranberries," she said.

On Saturday night, the moon rose behind indigo clouds. It had rained all day. She put on her dark clothes, gloves, and cap and her thin-soled climbing shoes, and she pulled boots over the shoes and a pair of socks over the boots. Then she went to her stash. Working by feel in the damp and dark, she laid out what she needed: the red-lensed flashlight, the dentist's mirror, the first-aid kit, the small drill and hacksaw, lockpicks, a pry bar, a linoleum knife, wire snips, magnetic wafers, a strobe light on a string, a double-angled slim jim with a suction cup on it, and her carabiners, rope, belay device and harness. She put the unused tools back into the pipe, sealed it and stashed it again, and she rolled the others up in a piece of cloth that she slung across her back alongside the rope—all except the strobe light, which she put around her neck in case she was discovered, and the flashlight, picks and magnets, which were distributed among her pockets. A misty rain, smelling of the shoreline, began to fall as she set off for the popshow district.

The side door on Lobelia Street had no handle. She cracked it with the pry and knife, slid in the jimmy and, using her left hand, depressed the push-bar. With her right hand she held a magnet against the spot on the door jamb where the alarm contact was located, advancing it to cover the switch at exactly the same rate that the door was opened. Once inside, although she had both the passcode and Skip's confirmation number, she did not disable the alarm. Instead, she progressed down the hallway in a manner that some-one standing nearby would not have perceived as walking; to the motion-sensitive cameras, she did not appear to be there at all. She moved incrementally, rolling the bones of her foot one by one off the floor, lifting the foot itself through space with the slowness of a clock's hour hand and lowering her heel to the floor seventy to eighty sec-onds later. She opened her mind to the pain in her legs and lived within it.

Three hours later she was in the men's room. Quickly now, working at the end of the row of urinals, she removed a metal plate from the wall, reached up inside the thicket of cables and, with the aid of the mirror, severed the camera connection. She replaced the plate, left the bathroom, gained the atrium in a few strides, climbed the rock face, and landed silently on the cushioned carpet of the tenth floor. The office of the chief executive was on the far side of the floor. Inside, she turned off the alarm. Behind the desk was a second door leading to Skip Stone's private studio apart-ment, where he sometimes brought girlfriends or spent the night. She listened with her ear against the wood.

Nothing; or a stillness that sounded like nothing. She opened the door and, for the first time that night, turned on her flashlight.

The apartment was spare. It contained no popshow and no furniture save a small wardrobe, a bedside table and a bed. A sliding door at one end revealed the bathroom. On the table was a tray with the remains of someone's dinner. A plastic fork angled up from the floor, its tines embed-ded in the carpet.

"I know you're in here," Sterling said. "I can see you under the bed."

The breathing seemed to stop momentarily, as though a small animal had expired in fear. She swept the light across the room and saw a tap-tap wedged upright into the track of the sliding door. It looked dented, evidently having been whacked repeatedly. "This can't take all night," she said. "We have twenty minutes until the police get here. Are you coming?"

There was no answer. Now she bent and looked. A pair of eyes stared back at her, glimmering in the red light. There was a long silence. "Nineteen minutes," Sterling said.

A guttural voice said, "Where?"

"Somewhere else."

There was no answer. Sterling turned off the flashlight and lay full-length on the floor, on her stomach. From here she could discern a small human shape in the same position. She said, "Let's go."

The voice croaked, "Are you a burglar?"

"No, I work here. Come on, move."

Slowly it wriggled free of the bed, making a scraping noise. It stood up and became a child of ten or eleven, dressed in pajamas, with a metal cylinder hanging from a string around its neck. "What is that?" Sterling said. The child made no answer, only clutched the thing to its chest. "Tuck it inside your shirt," she said.

The child did so. "Coming?" said Sterling. It nodded. "You have to do exactly as I say. Do you understand?"

It nodded again.

"Don't make one sound, or you could get us killed." A third miniscule nod. "Climb on my back."

She turned, squatting, and felt the creature clamber on. Her quads ached as she rose. On the way down the hall her feet fell too heavily, and only by considering herself an animal of almost two hundred pounds was she able to adjust her gait. She reached the balcony, pulled the rope from her side and looped it around a column, then fed it through the belay device on her belt with one hand while reaching for the child's bony ankles with the other. Obediently the child clamped her little arms around Sterling's collarbone as Sterling stepped up on the rail and swung them over.

The metal cylinder dug into her spine. She started to rappel, moving swiftly down the wall, her feet finding their way around the holds she had used on the way up. The child got heavier as they went down. Her breath was hot against Sterling's neck, and she smelled of strange artifice—plastic, paint and preservative. Her fists dug into Sterling's windpipe. Sterling wondered if her own arms would seize and pitch the two of them into the ficus plants at the foot of the atrium, where they would suffer their broken bones until the police arrived to shoot them both dead.

It was pouring outside. Rain ran in rivulets around Sterling's feet and lashed its fringed curtain against her face. Clutching the legs of her cargo, she jogged through streets she could hardly see. The child jolted on her back, holding on fanatically but still, true to her word or whatever fear bound her, making not the slightest sound.

She had made a big mistake.

"Thanks for coming over."

"Don't blame me if you all get arrested."

She was not going to prison. Prisoners were subjected to more popshow at louder volumes and higher resolutions than any other group in America. She had a stashed tap-tap full of identity documents. She had a contact in Caribbeantown who would put a chip in her arm.

"We could blame you, though, couldn't we?" Aimee said.

She didn't even need the fake ID. She could leave the country under her own name if she had to. After all, there was nothing to tie her to any act of sabotage committed in North Harbor. Nothing except the Negro urchin who now walked into the room, draped to the knees in a yellow T-shirt that said "Community Consumer Advocates," and stared at her.

"Do you want a sandwich, sweetie?"

The familiar head gave a terse shake. "My friend is here to see Lore," Aimee said. "Will you pass that along?"

The child turned and walked out. "She won't talk," said Aimee, "and she seems to hate me."

Sterling had no reply.

"Not that I'm not happy to have her here, but you could have said something. You could have given us a hint."

She was considering possible destinations. Cuba? Aimee went on: "I would probably hate me too. Do you know how they live on the other side? Lore's been telling us. They don't have electricity, heat, they don't even have potable water. They live like pioneers or something. Right over the wall. It's enough to make you sick."

"Where's Jamie?"

"At work. He's not thrilled that you did this, I have to tell you. He said he could lose his law license."

"Hm," she said without interest. All at once the bedroom door flew open and a figure collided with her. She went rigid, putting her arms up to protect herself, and found a person trying to throttle her in an embrace.

"Sorry, Lore, she's not so good at human contact."

The assailant stepped back, revealing herself to be a small woman, nearly a girl, with light-brown skin and a head of close-cropped hair. Her mouth turned down when she smiled, revealing startlingly yellow teeth and a missing bicuspid. Aimee said, "Lore Henry, this is Sterling Teacher."

"What?" Sterling said.

"Sterling Teacher, step into my parlor."

In the bedroom, shoes, plates, glasses, half-eaten bags of Lollysnax and clumps of clothing were scattered all over the floor. The bed had been pushed partway into the closet and enclosed in a tent of sheets and blankets. Lore went straight to a saucer on the bureau and picked up a joint. "Who are you?" Sterling said.

"I'm Aimee and Jamie's houseguest," the girl said. "You want?"

She declined. The rebel leader dragged deep and smiled again. She was skinny inside her ragged jeans and shirt. Her feet were bare, the toes curling up slightly, and her hands were bony and articulated and scarred, one with a patch of pale burned skin. "Thank you for bringing my baby home."

"Not home," said someone inside the tent.

"I didn't do it for you," Sterling said.

"Who did you do it for, Sterling Teacher?"

"Look, I don't know why Aimee told you my name, but it would be best for both of us if you just forgot it."

"Don't worry, she hasn't said anything," Lore said. "Except that you can get in and out of any building in this city without leaving a trace, and you don't like to talk to strangers."

She was never talking to Aimee again, that was for damn

sure. She turned to go, and the rebel leader said, "Reka wants to ask you something."

She pronounced it Ray-ka, and it sounded to Sterling like the name of some small demanding god. The child appeared between two sheets, sullen and wary-looking. Her eyes really were remarkably large, and as black as plums. She said in her croaking voice, "Can you take my pictures down?"

"No."

"Why not?"

"Because stealing you out of Coyson was feasible. Striking two hundred jumbos prominently located throughout the city is not feasible."

"What's feasible?"

"Practical," said Lore. "What about just one?"

"I don't have time to discuss this with you."

"I think you have the time," Lore said.

Sterling sat down. Abducting an urchin had been the worst-considered act of her career. It had unleashed a cluster of variables that were shooting off in all directions, like albumen streaming from a boiling egg whose shell, too late, is revealed to be full of holes. With her environment so disordered, there was nothing to do but wait. It would take years of caution and retrenchment before she could work again.

"How do I know you're not B.B.P.?" she said.

"What's that?"

"Police."

"If you thought we were, you wouldn't be asking."

That was true, but she said anyway, "I have no reason to trust you."

"Reka, baby, go see Aimee."

"No," the child said.

"I need to show Sterling something. Go on."

Reka thumped down from the bed, stomped out and slammed the door. Lore picked up the joint. "Sure you won't have some?" she said.

Sterling shook her head. Lore dragged, held the smoke in and finally released it, closing her eyes blissfully. "The best I've ever had," she said. "Everything here is the best. The mattress, my god. It's fucking paradise." She opened her eyes and beckoned to Sterling. "Come over here."

Sterling did. Why not? She stood before Lore as the girl started unbuttoning her shirt. Her ribcage was revealed, her small breasts, barely rounded, and one dark nipple so mutilated it looked split in half.

"I was tortured by SAPIDAD. What you call Sirocco. I was held for five months and tortured every few days. This is an electrical burn."

"Put your shirt on."

She drew the sides of the shirt back together, looking up at Sterling. Sterling was not tall, but Lore was shorter still. "Do you believe me?"

"What happened to you is not my responsibility."

"Of course not. Your responsibility is to your work."

The acuity of this took her aback. "Listen," Lore said, "can you get me back over the wall?"

"Absolutely not."

"Why?"

"That wall is sixteen stories high and a hundred and fifty miles long. It's almost a mile thick in some places. And there's an army inside."

"I got through," Lore said.

"How exactly?"

"As cargo. Locked in an ice chest."

Her saboteur's mind worked quickly. "That would take collaborators on the inside."

"The truck driver," Lore said, "and one of the customs inspectors. Not collaborators, good people who believe in the goals of our movement."

"And what are those?"

"Justice, Sterling Teacher," said the girl from SAPID. Again she inhaled the best marijuana smoke she'd ever tasted, looking like someone who had everything she needed in life. "Justice and peace."

⌒

Like the frog in the pot, she did not feel the element around her seething until it was too late—in Sterling's case, when she answered her door some hours later and saw Lore, drenched with midnight rain, wearing a hooded sweatshirt but otherwise undisguised.

"You've got to be kidding me."

"Can I come in? I'm freezing my ass off."

"How the fuck did you get here?"

"You're not the only one in this town who knows how to avoid the police," Lore said.

She was in the bathroom for a long time and emerged perfumed, beads of water riding her hair, in Sterling's thermal undershirt. Her dark areolas were visible through the damp white fabric. She said, "Do you have anything to eat?"

"Do you know how much danger you're putting me in?"

"How much?" Lore said. "Enough to send you back to SAPID to be sentenced for treason against the regime?"

Cheerfully, she helped herself to a hunk of salami and a jar of peanut butter. Sterling watched in disbelief as she dipped the first into the second and ate with apparent relish. "I tell you what, let me crash here tonight and I won't bother you again," she said. "It will be as though I had never been."

She prowled the room, picking up Sterling's things while finishing off the peanut butter with a fork. What was this? A clothes iron, said Sterling, what did it look like? Where was her, what was it called, her tap-tap? "I don't have one."

"Then how do you call people up?"

"I don't."

"What if Aimee wants to get in touch with you?"

"She manages somehow," Sterling said.

"Where's the other shit?"

"What other shit?"

"You know, the suction cups and catsuit and shit."

"First of all, I don't know what you're talking about," Sterling said. "And second, if you mention it again, you have to go."

"Why do you do it?" Lore asked.

"What did I just say?"

"Private between you and me," she said. She had been peering into Sterling's closet; she shut the door and turned around. "No fooling, now."

"Why do you care?"

"I'll tell you if you make us some coffee."

Why was everything a deal? "I have instant."

"Whatever you have, baby, it better by far than what we scrounge up on the other side."

She sat down on Sterling's only chair and waited. When the coffee came, she sniffed it with deep satisfaction. "Oh, you don't know," she said. "Carrot and beet root, you have no idea." She immediately drank half the cup, though it was burning hot. With her fuzzy skull and skinny limbs she looked like an ascetic on some unearthly high. "I gots to be taking some of this back, for sure."

The switch in lingo irked Sterling. "Just tell me why you care so much about what I do in my spare time."

"Because you do something. Everyone else around here just sits on their hands."

"Aimee and Jamie don't."

"We're talking about you now."

Years of training and self-preservation should have—in the past had always—sealed her lips. Yet she said, "I hate it."

"Hate what?"

"Popshow. I hate it. All right?"

"Why?"

"It gets in my head."

"Invades?"

"I guess."

"Occupies?"

"What's your point?"

Lore finished her coffee. "Have you ever thought about the chain of supply?" she said.

"Meaning?"

"The manufacturing process. Where all these goods come from, that popshow is supposed to make you covet."

"They come from SAPID."

"How do you feel about that?"

Sterling shrugged. Lore looked at her curiously. "Ninety percent of consumer goods in North Harbor are made by exploited labor," she said. "That doesn't bother you?"

"I don't buy them."

"What about your iron?"

"Trash," Sterling said.

"Your clothing?"

"Trash."

"Your tools?"

"What tools?" Sterling said. She took Lore's cup. "You can sleep on the floor."

She woke in early morning to find Lore at the window. Her slight form was motionless, shrouded in curtains and outlined by the glow of jumbos. Sterling lay watching for about five minutes. When she spoke, Lore gave a violent start that almost jerked the curtains from their rod.

"If you don't care about your own safety, at least have some consideration for mine."

The room was alight, as usual, with gliding tranches of color and buzzed with the bass rumble of the hypes outside. Through this magic-lantern show moved the apparition of the unwelcome visitor, pausing at the side of the bed.

"Can I get in?"

What a ridiculous idea, said Sterling's thoughts, but they were far away. She felt herself sinking into the bed. The apparition stood above her, undressing: first the shirt was pulled up and away, then the shorts dropped to the floor. Lights passed over her body, calling out its bones. She took the sheet and drew it down the length of the bed, away from Sterling. The mattress dipped like a ship as she mounted it and turned her articulate fingers on Sterling, removing her clothes. Sterling's skin crawled upon her, flinching with the violence of Lore's own fear, trying to shrink from the touch but not succeeding. She heard the sibilant exhalation of steady breath and realized Lore was calming her, singing to her between her teeth, like one of them was a child or a fretful sister.

Day 15

She would have been killed if anybody opened that case of champagne. As it was, the next time she was arrested she would be sent immediately, without trial, to long-term detention. She was on a fifty-person watch list issued by SAPIDAD (although this was the only truth, she told Sterling, amused, to the idea that she was a "rebel leader"). And all she wanted to do in North Harbor was give a speech.

"That's it?"

"That's all."

"Why couldn't you get somebody else to give it for you? Jamie's a public defender. He loves making speeches."

"Don't you think there's an advantage to a personal appearance?" said Lore.

Sterling, who had dealt with that advantage three nights running, said nothing. Lore turned to Aimee. "Did you talk to your friend at the institute?"

"She'll be there. She's meeting with other stakeholders tomorrow."

"You should give them a place to put their stakes down," Sterling said. Aimee frowned and went on: "We have commitments from the North Harbor Working Group on Corporate Governance, Citizens for Social Responsibility, and Parents Rating Popshow."

"A stake-check, as it were."

"Jamie's bringing people from Legal Aid, and I have a tap in to the Harbor Bay Housing Coalition."

"That's wonderful, Aim," Lore said. "How's Reka?"

Not great.

This was the second day Lore had spent in Sterling's apartment, and she was settled right in—eating a sandwich of cream cheese and tuna fish and drinking her third cup of coffee, taking notes by hand on an old pad of wrinkled paper Aimee had found her and generally making Sterling's life a misery.

"Tell me more," she said that night. "Tell me about the first time."

Sterling refused. In fact it had been an idiotic attempt to vandalize Advent, a small firm on Poplar Street, nearly fifteen years ago. She had broken her leg jumping off the fire escape. "It's none of your business."

"Oh, Sterling Teacher, you are my business."

"If you want to fuck—"

"I can't wait," said Lore, dropping her voice in a way that sent a rush of unwelcome sensation through Sterling's body. She gritted her teeth and said, "We can do that, but don't ask questions."

"Did you learn by yourself, or did somebody teach you?"

"Do you not have ears?"

"Do you use assistants, or do you work alone?" She left her papers on the bed. "How do you get inside buildings? Do you climb through the window? Can you jump across rooftops? Have you ever been caught?"

She straddled Sterling on the floor, holding herself up on her knees so that their skin did not touch. Her body was all points—nipples, collarbone, pelvis—and Sterling thrust her torso upward, trying to make contact with them. She managed to hook Lore with her legs and pulled her down. They lay naked against each another. Lore moved slowly, pressing all her points into Sterling, whose arousal felt like a net of flame which if drawn tighter would slice her apart. When it was over she rolled Lore onto the floor and finger-fucked her with cold, calculated strokes, or so she thought, until she found herself filled with warm currents that trembled and exploded on her own fingertip when she touched her soaking crotch.

They crawled into bed. Lore lay on her back, flinging out her arms in satisfaction and accidentally hitting Sterling across the chest. "Maybe I'll take *you* back with me," she said.

"No, thanks."

"Why not? Good people, good work and all the sex you can eat."

"Terrorism, gang warfare, gun battles in the streets."

"Look here," said Lore. She tapped her own solar plexus. "This is your terrorist. And the police are worse than any gang."

"And the gun battles?"

"It's not a battle if only one side has guns."

"You people don't have guns?"

"We're committed to nonviolent revolution."

"That's the dumbest thing I've ever heard."

She leaned above Sterling on her elbow. Sweat still stood on her forehead and under her lip, gleaming in the play of popshow. Her skin smelled not of roses and chlorine, as Aimee's always had—Sterling had not known she remembered the scent—but of cumin, bitter chrysanthemums, and pot. She caressed Sterling's cheek with her thumb for a moment before Sterling jerked her head away. "Oh, it's like that?" Lore said.

"I'll sleep on the floor."

She put her hand flat on Sterling's chest. "You sleep right fucking here."

She lay down again and said, "Every revolution conceived in violence has ended in violence. You can't end the cycle of pain and destruction by causing more pain."

"But you can get yourself killed and have it all be for nothing."

"Yes and no," Lore said.

Violence by its nature was brittle, creating brittle kingdoms. Love was transformative. It grew beyond the individual people who practiced it and took on a tangible existence at the heart of a movement, where it knit everyone together in a way no human being could do.

"You sound like a romance longshow," Sterling said.

"You sound like someone wrapped up in hate."

"What are you going to do, go up to the Sirocco troops and love them? I'm sure that'll bring down the wall."

"We don't need your endorsement, Teacher. You stick

to blowing up billboards."

"You think that's what I do?" Sterling said. "Blow shit up?"

"Blow shit up, hit shit, it all the same when your basic purpose is misguided."

"I've caused more problems for Sirocco than your entire movement."

"Is that so?" Lore said. "How much of a problem do you think you've caused?"

"Over a billion dollars' worth of damage. From their own figures."

"Oh, my."

"One billion dollars—you think that doesn't make a dent?"

"What was Sirocco's net profit last year?"

Sterling shrugged. Lore put her hands over her face and sighed. "Give me your tap-tap," she said.

"You know I don't have a fucking tap-tap."

"Then do this in your fucking head. Last year's profit was forty-five trillion dollars. How many billions is that?"

"I don't know."

"How many, Teacher?"

"Forty-five thousand."

"And one billion is what fraction of forty-five thousand billion?"

She said resentfully, "Point oh oh … oh oh two."

"Two one-thousandths of a percent. And you're not doing a billion dollars' worth of damage every year, are you? You've been at it about ten years. Right? So if you take their total profit over that period, which is roughly two hundred and seventy trillion dollars from their *own* figures, and divide that into a billion, what percent have you cost them?"

"Fine," Sterling said.

"A couple of ten-thousandths of a percent. Not enough to cross the threshold of materiality, Sterling. Not even enough to keep a junior accounting clerk up at night."

"I'm not trying to demolish the entire company," she pointed out. "If I wake up the day after a hit and half the jumbos in the city have gone dark, I did my job."

"Has that ever happened?"

"Of course."

"How long did it take them to come back up?"

"Two hours."

"And how many years did you prep for that hit?"

"Look, what do you want from me? I'm fighting the fight I woke up in," Sterling said. "We can't all be behind the wall."

"That is very true," Lore said. "But you can."

"Excuse me?"

"You think you're accomplishing shit over here? Pummelling away with your little hits, your little secret missions? Let me tell you something, you scratching a tank with your fingernails. You keep on scratching and scratching, and it keep rolling right on over you. You all like, 'I'm making my dent—I'm making my dent here,' and you don't even notice you buried up to ya neck in the ground."

"You know what would happen if I somehow got into SAPID? I'd be shot on sight."

"And your life so worthwhile, right? You got some meaningful work right here. And a million friends."

"Fuck you, Lore."

"Oh, so you know my name? You fuck me and let me suck your pussy and I'm nobody, but one piece of criticism and suddenly we on a first-name basis?"

"Why did you even come here? Are you deliberately trying to fuck up my life?"

"Oh, yeah. Half the people in SAPID are working ninety-hour weeks in stinking, unsafe factories where they don't have the right to organize or even go to the bathroom, and the other half are out there fighting occupation by our own government and trying not to starve to death. And half of them is in prison. My people are dropping like flies and my chief concern in this life is whether you, Sterling, get out of your bourgeois head or not."

"You need to leave."

"You carried that baby in your arms," she said, getting out of bed. "And God knows you seen all of me, but just go on telling yourself we don't exist."

"I'll get your clothes." They were both grabbing for them when somebody knocked on the door. Sterling pushed Lore into the bathroom. She scrambled into her own clothes and listened. A man's voice said, "Sterling?"

She said stupidly, "Cleveland?"

"That's me."

"It's the middle of the night."

"Three o'clock, actually!" came his cheerful voice.

"What do you want?"

"What? I can't hear you."

"I said what the hell do you want?"

"What?"

She opened the door. "What the fucking hell do you want?" she said. Cleveland was standing in the hallway with a white paper bag in one hand and a tap-tap, raised to her eye level, in the other. The screen read:

BUREAU OF BRAND PROTECTION
DEPARTMENT OF CRIMES AGAINST
CORPORATE INTEGRITY

Joint Task Force on Subversion
William C. Eddy, *Agent-in-Charge*

"Who the fuck is William C. Eddy?"

"Who do you think?" he said. He held up the bag. "Would you like some Lollynuts?"

"You work for the B.B.P.?"

"Funny," he remarked, "most people say, 'You're B.B.P.?' As if my existence was coterminous with the Bureau's."

"You need a warrant to come in here."

Still holding the paper bag, he lifted one finger and tapped up a document. She read, *Agent W. Eddy having appeared before me and made oath that he has good ground and reason to believe, and does believe that there is now concealed on these premises.* "Please let me in," Agent W. Eddy said.

She stood aside. He wore short sleeves, and she saw for the first time that he was smooth-skinned and muscular, and that without the beaming smile his face was sharp. His amber curls caught the light as he seated himself in her only chair. "Why don't you take the bed?" he suggested.

She sat among the creased and dampened sheets. From the white bag, Agent Eddy produced a couple of plump Lollynuts and two hot-drink cups. "I thought we'd like something to nosh on as we continued our little conversation," he said. "The tea is Secret Pasha. Do you prefer Lemon-Forsythia or MintRGreen?"

"Why are you here?"

"For the same reason I took you out to lunch, Sterling. I want to get to know you better."

"Then why do you have a warrant?"

"Oh, that's a formality," Cleveland said. "It worked, though, didn't it?"

She was horribly distracted. Her body was making itself felt: the muscle fatigue in her arms, an aching tenderness in her cunt. It was hard to concentrate on Cleveland, even though he was directly opposite her. Her mind kept slipping to the bathroom door and to the sower of chaos behind it.

"There are things you don't know about me. Besides the obvious one that we've disposed of, I mean. I genuinely like you, Sterling, and I admire your work. I may be able to help you here."

I am going to kill her, she thought, kill her and then throw her out. Then it occurred to her that Lore was working in tandem with Cleveland. Why else would he have arrived at the moment when she was least capable of rational thought? She almost got up and hauled Lore out of the bathroom. Cleveland was looking at her as if he expected a response. She said, "I have no idea what you're talking about."

With a small sigh, he handed her the tea. "I was hoping we could come to a position of mutual respect."

"I have no respect for you."

"Yet the role I play is just as challenging, in its way, as yours," he said. He sipped his tea, surveying the room. "This is nice. Spartan. I suppose the accoutrements are off-site?"

"The what?"

"Accoutrements. You know, like suction cups and catsuits?"

Rage surged up in her, more powerful than an orgasm. "Didn't she tell you?"

He only raised his eyebrows.

"What's the point of having two of you if you don't fucking communicate with each other? Do I have to do everything twice? Are you going to fuck me too?" She was on her feet, throwing open the bathroom door. In the blinding incandescence of her anger she glimpsed Lore perched on the tub's edge. When she turned around, Cleveland too had gotten to his feet and was peering into the bathroom with an expression of utter amazement.

"Miss Henry," he said. "You're a long way from home."

Lore was awake. Sterling hoped she wouldn't start talking again. She had spent yesterday having at Sterling relentlessly, not for her betrayal (although for that Sterling felt a certain unaccustomed remorse) but for refusing to join the revolution. Being identified by a federal agent and narrowly escaping arrest had apparently only made Lore more committed to her impossible mission of getting Sterling over the wall.

"You won't believe how good you feel. It'll be like breathing fresh air for the first time."

"See what your fresh air has brought me. Goons outside my window and a date with Cleveland."

"Ah, but that's all your own doing, ain't it? Those are your own actions come back at you."

"So if I join your revolution, I won't ever have to deal with the police?"

"Listen to me, Sterling. What I'm saying is it don't matter if you have to deal with the police. When you live a life of complete openness, when you open your heart to the love of the world, the police can't touch you."

"Like they didn't touch you."

"You missing the forest for the trees."

"You're missing the trees for the forest fire."

"There is a fire," Lore said. "It's a fire of hatred, and it's consuming you. But look here, Sterling. I'm standing right where you are. I am in the flames with you, and I am not consumed."

Cleveland had promised her twenty-four hours to complete and deliver her speech. After that, he said, he could not be responsible for her safety. She seemed happy with this, in the overly trusting way that sometimes made Sterling wonder if she was touched in the head.

"How can you believe him?" Sick as she was of having Lore around, it infuriated her that she would so blithely throw away her freedom. "Do you think he really gives a shit about you?"

"I don't know. But I give a shit about him."

"Great. Now we're both tied to his balls because you've got some fucked-up idea about loving your enemies."

"It's not an idea, it's a practice," Lore said. "And I think the reason we tied to his balls is that nasty temper you got on you."

"He's been in my hair for nine months," Sterling said. "God! Laughing at me the entire time."

"Well, you got to admit you gave him a lot to laugh about."

By the time they went to bed they were not speaking to each other. And when Lore woke in the early morning, she did not speak. She lay with her limbs locked rigid, breathing in harsh rasps separated by seconds of strangled silence. Her skin was hot, and the passing lights showed it to be wet. A rank and fetid smell came off her. Sterling had the feeling that to touch her would be to electrocute one of them. So she looked at her, not moving herself, until the rigidity seemed to overtake her too and she fell uneasily asleep.

She dreamed she was carrying something on her back through pale, windowless corridors without end. The floors in her dream were old, of closely lain, narrow hardwood boards polished to a gloss and secured here and there with ancient rivets and lumps of sodder, but the walls were cheap pressboard, painted white with large stylized orange numbers representing the floor levels. She passed through a pair of large trundle doors, battered seven-foot slabs that slid on iron tracks embedded in the floor. The thing she was carrying weighed almost nothing—she could feel its crooked bones. Delicate hands embraced her neck, and a voice said in her ear, "Have you ever thought about the chain of supply?"

In daylight, Cleveland came to take Sterling to brunch. He explained that he had been watching her for some time. "Not as closely as this last semester, of course. Which has been a very rewarding experience, by the way."

"Do you literally get a reward?"

"We're not white slavers, Sterling," he said reprovingly. "My career has actually suffered over the years because of you."

"Glad to hear it."

"I was told repeatedly not to waste my time. My last promotion was contingent on my forgetting all about the sabotage cases."

"And you kept your word."

"You'll find I'm not a company man," Cleveland said. "Not all the way through."

Sterling ate her GinghamFreshFarms egg. It was a long time since she had experienced food as anything but a system of nourishment interrupted by branding, and today was no different, although Cleveland had chosen a very expensive restaurant. "You have no evidence," she said.

"I have probable cause."

"Not the same thing."

"Your confession in the apartment."

"Hardly."

"As a matter of fact, both are more than enough to keep you under surveillance indefinitely."

"I doubt that," Sterling said.

"If you know Miss Henry," said Cleveland, "then you know a little bit about our reach. It's not exercised in the same way over here, of course, but it's not something you should dismiss."

She remembered something Lore had said to him: "Sooner or later, there will be a reckoning. You'll need to decide where you stand."

"How do you know her?" she asked.

"I've been in the field," he said. "Off and on."

"I'm surprised you haven't gotten singed."

"Pardon?"

"From standing in the flames with her."

Cleveland frowned. "Would you like to hear how I narrowed it down to you?" he said.

"No."

Delicately he lifted his Frangipani Blueberry Mimosa. The restaurant was so expensive that there was no pop-show on the walls, and his L-shaped cufflinks shone unmolested in a clear azure light. "Well, there's plenty of time," he said.

He drove her home, the detail following in a tan sedan. "They can't go into private buildings, but they'll be stationed at all the exits," Cleveland said. "I'm thinking five to six at a time, in ten-hour shifts."

"How long can you keep that up?"

"As I said, Sterling, until we have the evidence to convict you."

"What if there is no evidence?"

"Then I guess we'll be watching you for the rest of your life."

She went inside, climbed to the roof, jumped onto the next building and effortlessly lost them. Half an hour later she was in Caribbeantown, ringing the bell of an apartment above a lock shop on Amaranth Avenue. When the inhabitant saw who it was he tried to shut the door in her face. "I want my dog," she said.

"You have the wrong address."

"You bred that dog to my specifications, I gave you twenty thousand dollars, now I want my fucking dog."

"It's too late, Jane," her contact said. He peered past her into the hall. "That agent's been here. The one with the teeth."

"Fuck!" Sterling said. She took a step away, to master herself. The chipper watched with a trace of sympathy. "You're done, huh?" he said.

"That fucking pansy."

"Well, I'm sorry. You had a good run."

"You better hope I don't take you with me," she said.

Cleveland was parked outside the lock shop. "Nice visit?" he said out the passenger window.

"I have a right to go for a walk."

"You certainly do. Get in the car."

She stared forward while he navigated the narrow streets. "Let me explain this to you," he said. "I don't give a damn who your associates are. I don't give a damn for your little escape plans. It doesn't bother me that you're harboring a notorious insurgent in your apartment. What I care about, and what I will work ceaselessly to ensure, is that you never break into a building in North Harbor again."

"It must be nice, enjoying the fruits of your labor. Keeping the people of SAPID down so that you can have all the Lollysocks and Lollyties your little heart desires."

"Don't be ridiculous," Cleveland said. He turned onto her street. "The people of SAPID are nothing to either of us."

The floor of the apartment was strewn with paper, and Lore was asleep in the middle of it. She lay in a compact and protective position, one arm bent beneath her head and the other thrust between her drawn-up knees. Sterling nudged her with the side of a shoe. "Hey," she said, "we have beds here."

Lore woke at once. "How was breakfast?"

"Humiliating."

She began to gather the papers, yawning. "If you go over, you won't have to kowtow to Cleveland."

"You're asking me to commit suicide," Sterling said. Suddenly fatigued, she lay down on the bed. "I admit things could be better, but I'm not about to exterminate myself."

"I'm asking you to commit to life."

It was annoying that she needed no warm-up: one minute she was sleeping like a vagrant on a park bench, the next she was on Sterling's back again. "Just tell me one thing," Sterling said.

"Will you promise to go over?"

"No!"

"Think about it. *Think*," Lore said.

"I'm thinking I'm not about to abandon a life where I have food, shelter, money and medical care for a war zone where I would get shot, lynched, have a bomb dropped on me or get thrown in a Sirocco prison."

"Your loss."

"Why are you riding my ass so hard? That's what I want to know. What do you care about me? Why don't you bother yourself about Reka—she's the one who really needs help."

"Reka has help."

"Why am I the soul you have to save?"

Lore didn't answer. Sterling watched her shuffle her notes into order. "What happened last night?" she asked.

"What do you think happened?"

"Love didn't help you," Sterling said. "When they were doing those things to you. Did it? It didn't get you out of there, did it?"

Lore looked up, coldly. "There's something about you," she said, "I don't know what, that makes you the ignorantest, most pigheaded bastard I ever tried to teach. And I have known me some ignorant motherfuckers."

"Tell me. What did love do for you then?"

"It kept me alive, you ignant child. It kept me from becoming them."

Day 18

"Thank you for coming. My name is Lore Henry."

The church was small and drafty. It was almost June, but the weather in North Harbor was as inclement as it had been all spring. Scattered in the pews were about forty nonprofit types: women with graying hair and silver jewelry, lean men in blazers and old ties.

"To those I haven't met, and I haven't been able to meet as many of you as I would have wished, I'd like to extend a special welcome. You're probably here because Aimee leaned on you to come—"

They laughed.

"—and I want you to know how truly grateful I am for your attention this morning.

"As I said, my name is Lore Henry. I'm twenty-two years old, and I was forcibly emigrated into SAPID, with the rest of my family, when I was three. Six years ago, my father and mother were murdered by Sirocco and dumped at my front door in body bags. We were later invoiced for the body bags." She paused. "It's okay to laugh at that."

There was one nervous male guffaw. "I did," Lore said. "But I also wanted to die. I went away to die, and it took me a long time to come back."

Although she was standing on a footstool behind the podium, she was visible only from the shoulders up. She had a page of notes that she was not consulting. "Again, I've been lucky enough to meet and talk with some of you, and those conversations have been, for me, uniformly thought-provoking and encouraging; I hope you feel the same. I have shared with some of you my purpose in coming to North Harbor and what I hope to accomplish here. But right now, if you'll permit me, I'd like to start by telling you why I'm not here."

At the back of the room, beside Sterling, Aimee and Jamie were debating in whispers. Jamie looked like he was trying to keep his temper. Aimee's usually round, milky face was slack and blotched with red. "It's crazy," she whispered. "It's like putting up a neon jumbo right over her head."

"If we get the injunction—"

"If?" she said, forgetting to whisper. A woman in front of them turned around and asked them to be quiet.

Lore had claimed never to have used a microphone, but her voice came clear and expertly to their ears. "I'm not here to take your money," she was saying. "Many of you have asked me what we need and how you can donate. Your generosity has been overwhelming. But say you tried—say my friend Rose Rosenbaum tried to give me ten thousand dollars today."

Rose Rosenbaum was apparently an old lady in the front row. Sterling could just see her tiny shoulders. She wondered how Lore had managed to meet all these luminaries. "How would she do that?" Lore said. "How would you do that, Rose?"

The old woman's voice sounded like the chirping of a bird. "Well, I'd try tapping it to you."

"And of course that wouldn't work, because I don't have a tap-tap."

"*If* you get the injunction," Aimee whispered savagely, "*maybe* they won't come and take her away." Sterling poked her in the side, and got a swift poke back. "What's wrong with you?" she whispered to Aimee, who said without whispering, "What's wrong with *you*?"

"I'd write a check!" said the perky little voice of Rose Rosenbaum. From the dais Lore said, "But I don't have a bank account. Nobody in SAPID does, except military and government personnel. Also, SAPID has its own reserve. Checks written over here are useless there."

"Cash," someone called out.

"The first time I used it, I'd be hunted down, beaten up and robbed—if not by my own people, then by the police."

The audience was out of ideas. "I'm not here for money," Lore said. "Our movement needs a lot of things, but it doesn't need money right now."

She stopped and requested water. A bottle was handed forward, and Lore came around the podium for it. "Thank you so much," she said, sounding young and unprotected without the microphone. In a low voice, Jamie said to Aimee, "Our advisors agreed this was the best strategy."

"Well, your advisors are bonkers."

"Another thing I'm not here to do. I'm not here to make you feel bad. Look, the truth about SAPID is hard, and when we are faced with hard truths, it's human nature to avoid them. When you hear that ninety-nine percent of all permanent residents in SAPID live below the federal poverty line; when you hear that the infant mortality rate in SAPID is eight percent—which, by the way, is three points higher than the infant mortality rate in Bangladesh; when you hear that adult life expectancy in SAPID is sixty years old for women and fifty-five for men, and falling; when you hear that diseases like dysentery, typhoid, and cholera, diseases that were eliminated a century ago in most developed nations ..."

Aimee would not let it drop. "How in the world do you get from protecting a child to suing a popshow house?"

"I've explained this. Since she has no standing—"

"Excuse me, I get that you're having an important discussion?" said the woman in front of them. "I appreciate that? But can you take it outside?"

Aimee stood up and, grabbing Sterling's wrist, nudged Jamie out of his seat. As they made their way down to the aisle, Lore was saying: "Fear is dehumanizing, it makes us feel small. So we have a reaction to the reaction. We want to attack someone, or we want to hide. This is called fight or flight, and it kept us safe when we were living in caves. So if you're sitting here feeling any of these things, if you feel guilty, if you feel angry at me, if you feel despair— especially despair—please believe me, these are all natural reactions. They're a side effect of my being here, but they are not *why* I'm here."

The sanctuary door slammed. The three of them were in the lobby at the front of the church. "I'm really troubled by you," Aimee said. "I see this, this ambition all of a sudden. I feel like you're riding to success on this little girl's back."

James O'Bannon was a medium-sized guy, not bad-looking, with blue eyes almost the same color as Aimee's and a tattoo of blind Justice on his arm. He'd been an anarchist when Aimee first met him, one of those rabble-rousing anti-Partition types she adored, though she didn't sleep with him until ten years later. Afterwards she tapped Sterling in tears, asking if she could still be a lesbian, when Sterling neither knew nor cared.

"Your friend"—he indicated Sterling—"arrived at our house before dawn last Sunday, carrying a minor child" (this and subsequent points he emphasized by holding up an index finger) "whom she then left in our care, without permission, without advising us that this minor was prominently featured on local jumbos, certainly without advising us that this minor was in North Harbor illegally. Which leaves us in the very difficult position of trying to advocate for that minor while corporate and government interests are probably tracking her, and us, down right this second."

"You need to take your finger out of my face."

"Since then I have spent every free moment studying case law, trying to dream up an escape hatch for all of us. So don't ever say I'm in this for personal gain."

"This isn't case law, Jamie. It's a child's life."

"What do you want me to do, Aimee? Do you want me to pick her up on my back and cart her away to Namibia?"

"Why do you say Namibia?" said Aimee, blinking very fast. "Do you think all black people are supposed to live in Africa?"

"Don't even go there with me. Don't go there. I've been in the work since you were six years old." They stared at each other, Aimee with an appalled, desperate expression, Jamie flushed to his dark hair. Sterling discovered in herself a mild curiosity about what Lore might be saying next.

"Can we go back in?" she said.

A current of cold air reached her. She turned and saw the heavy wooden doors to the street opening to admit a police officer. Another came in, then another, then five more. "Oh, my God," Aimee said. Police filled the lobby. Someone opened the sanctuary door. They heard Lore saying, "My future depends on it, and so does the future of every person in SAPID. We have far too much respect for the rule of law ever to ask someone to violate it."

The policemen began to file past into the church. Without hesitation, Lore's voice said, "So if I'm not here to scare you, take your money, make you shout things at a rally, or trick you into breaking the law, why am I here?"

The crush in the lobby eased, and Sterling saw that the police were entering the church two by two like dancers in a musical, parting at the font and moving into the side aisles. Soon there were a dozen policemen lined up on either side of the sanctuary. Everybody turned around or craned their necks, and sounds of alarm rose from the pews. "I'm here," Lore said, "to ask you to do the one thing we can't do for ourselves. Good morning, officers."

Something closed on Sterling's arm—Aimee's hand, clutching convulsively. "Good morning, ma'am," said a man midway up the room.

"Officer, my name is Lore Henry. Can I ask you for yours?"

"Sergeant Rider, ma'am. North Harbor Peace Patrollers LLC."

"Thank you, Sergeant Rider. And can I ask why you're here?"

"Just upholding the laws of the land, ma'am."

Sterling followed Aimee and Jamie back inside. The nonprofit managers in the pews were clearly uneasy but, just as clearly, found it difficult to believe they were in danger. Slowly all gazes reverted to Lore. She said, "Would you permit anyone who feels uncomfortable to leave at this time?"

The sergeant assented to this. Lore repeated that anyone who wished to could leave the building. At first nothing happened. "You may feel absolutely free," she said, and that encouraged a few souls to scurry out. "So." She lifted her head and seemed to smile at them all, from police to audience to Sterling at the back of the room. "So, what is it we cannot do for ourselves? At the risk of being arcane, I'm going to take it backwards again and start by telling you what we can do."

Another person got up and left.

"For now, because of our situation, the movement relies on quiet direct actions. But in the future—and this is why I say my future, and that of everyone in SAPID, depends on the law—in the future we are going to use the courts. You may know that SAPID is governed by an interim constitution. You may also know that this constitution was passed in a plebiscite that was called just twenty-four hours in advance and marred with extreme fraud."

At this point the sergeant warned her. He spoke less audibly than before, but Lore seemed to understand. "You're right," she said. "Sergeant Rider has reminded me that what I'm saying could be interpreted as incitement. But it is a fact that permanent residents of SAPID have no legal standing to challenge any provisions of this constitution in court. If a challenge is to be made, therefore, it has to be filed in North Harbor. But that's not what I'm asking you to do.

"The one thing we need, the one single thing the permanent residents of SAPID cannot provide for ourselves, is publicity. There is an official news blackout on every possible story coming out of SAPID. That wall between us is the wall between everyone in North Harbor and the truth."

"Ma'am, this is potential criminal defamation."

"Nobody in North Harbor, except the people in this room, knows what the movement in SAPID is accomplishing. Nobody in North Harbor knows that people are risking their lives every day in peaceful resistance, or that work in the factories is slowing down, or that the people of SAPID are educating each other and learning to work together."

One line of policemen began to ripple. It was Sergeant Rider picking his way past his colleagues to the front of the room. When he arrived at the piano, he unholstered his gun.

Five or six people made for the side door. Without any change of expression, Lore turned to the man and said, "Sergeant, are you going to shoot anyone in this audience?"

"I wouldn't do that, ma'am."

"Are you going to shoot me?"

"I'm just taking precautions, ma'am."

"I appreciate your honesty, Sergeant." She addressed the audience: "My friends, you are completely safe. This guardian of the peace is only here for me. Please, if you feel you can, honor me with your trust and stay just a few minutes more."

For the first time, she looked down at her notes. For a second she seemed to have lost her place.

"I'm not asking you to smuggle reporters across the border. We can get the stories out to you. We can get you photographs, video, audiotape. But that's not why I'm here. All that I ask, and the entire reason for my visit to your city, is that you go out and tell the truth about us. Tell your family, your neighbors, your co-workers, tell the guard in the subway station. Tell your old third-grade teacher and your refrigerator repairman. Tell people you meet at cocktail parties, tell people you meet in the gym. If every one of you here tells one person tonight, and asks them to tell one person more, the awareness will start happening and our work is halfway done."

Soft moaning sounds were coming from Aimee. More policemen ascended to the platform and clustered around Sergeant Rider.

"I'm making it sound easy. But it's not. Even here, even safe in North Harbor, opening your mouth and telling people the truth carries a tiny bit of risk. And you won't want to take that risk. You will be afraid. You may feel bad about yourself for being afraid. You may be angry at me for putting you on the spot, after I spent all this time promising that I wouldn't. You may think I'm a liar. You may hate me. You will be filled with doubt.

"Unfortunately, my time is short. So I'll say just one more thing. All those feelings are good feelings. They belong to you, so be proud of them, and love them. Love your own doubts and fears and your weaknesses and your anger. We all have them. We are all alike. For every one of us, when we manage to love ourselves, we begin to understand how to love others. And then the work is done. Thank you."

She stepped away from the podium, and Sergeant Rider moved in front of her. He was bigger than she was, so the audience could not see exactly what was happening, but there seemed to be a brief discussion and then Lore walked off toward the knot of policemen. One of them took her by the arm, the rest closed in, and she was shown out through a door to the left of the altar. Rider leaned into the microphone, saying, "Ladies and gentlemen, this has been an example of freedom of speech. We are shutting down the church now due to the fire code. Please exit peacefully and do not run."

"Oh, God, where are they taking her?" Aimee cried. The policemen worked their way around the room, speaking reassuringly, aiding the peaceable exit. "Jamie, what should we do?" He took her hand, led her towards the doors. "Tap me," she called to Sterling. The nonprofit managers rose, pretending to talk casually to one another. In five minutes they were gone.

Sterling went outside to the empty parking lot. She looked around the tarmac for a tan sedan, but it was not there. A breeze bent the tall, thin poplars at the margin of the parking lot, and a few individual raindrops began to fall. She looked for her police detail, for any sign of them, for Cleveland. But there was nothing.

II

QUEEN RAT

Onions

The court is becoming a nuisance. They squabble all
the time, and when they don't squabble they bicker. It's a
relief to be by herself, checking on her vegetables.

She got an early start today. The smell of spring, which
is damp and sharp like scallions, reached her even in bed.
Now the chocolate-dark mud clings to her feet as she
skirts the cemetery. You don't go into the cemetery, just
as you don't go into the woods. In either case you might
never come out, but the cemetery is, at the moment, more
awful to Reka, because she's heard that some people have
started digging up the graves. She really doesn't want to
meet those people. She doesn't want to meet anybody, in
fact, except the Traveler and of course her grandmother.
Sometimes she daydreams of being reunited with Alouette and crowning her with pearls, diadems, cornichons.
Actually, she's not sure about the cornichons. Tonight at
lessons she will look it up.

In the scrub between the graveyard and the woods she
keeps a small wild-looking garden. She stoops over it, and
the bag with her empty jug inside slides up and smacks
her on the back of the neck. She staggers around a little,
amusing herself, before going back to the garden. Pushing up the sleeves of her parka and her three sweaters and
her sweatshirt and her undershirt, she scratches away the
soil around feather-tops waving in the wind. The ground
is still cold enough to freeze her fingers, so she pulls out
her hands and presses them against her mouth and blows
on them. She can smell the thawing dirt. She tries again
and manages to loosen a carrot. There it is! A carrot! It's
half-frozen too but she can't wait, she dusts off the blind

little tail and puts it in her mouth, sucking it like a pop-sicle. When she bites down she does something bad to one of her teeth but she doesn't even care.

Before she leaves, she takes off the parka and some of her sweaters and slings on the bag—now full of carrots and onions—and puts her clothes back on over it. The cemetery and forest are quiet. Far off in the distance she can hear a moaning, oceanic sound that may be a vehicle accelerating on some remaining road. The sky is shining, so bright you can't look at it, and she doesn't know the word for that particular shade of blue. Above the trees, a thread of smoke sluggishly rises and is lost in the brilliance.

All at once she wants to climb the firehouse tower. She and her ladies will have a picnic, young tender ... vealets in pastry and cornichons (it's a pickle, she thinks now) and deviled eggs and jelly beans and wine. She picks her way along the edge of the woods, taking care not to stray into the trees, and across a stretch of shattered tarmac to the firehouse. Strands of dead ivy hang from its yellow bricks and the rivets on its heavy bolted doors are turning to rust. Sometimes people live here, but not often as the roof is mostly gone. She sticks her head into the tower doorway and listens. Now the steps. She has counted them: there are fifty-three. The stairwell smells of dead mouse. The tall slots in the walls let in plenty of sunlight, so she's not afraid. At the top she puts her whole head out one of the slots. The air is fresh and cold, and she can see the park spread out below her like a ragged brown wool blanket. It's so clear that she can see the brittle clustered lances of dead cattails, and the trampled-down paths leading through the rushes to the swamp, and even a bit beyond that to the blunt tops of the housing project, which glitter in the sun like something forgiven.

She turns around and looks out the back of the tower, towards her house. She can't see it, of course, but she can make out the chipped rim of the overpass; between here and there is the ramble of eroded roads, abandoned excavations, collapsed chain-link fencing, uprooted trees (something she hates to see) and the odd intact house that makes up what used to be a neighborhood. To her right are the woods. They're said to be full of drug addicts and Kidlanders, but they look airy and empty from up here, and there's an old stone comfort station among the trees—she can see its miniature battlements through the branches. She lays her cheek on her folded arms. The sun is right on her face, warming her skin and making a dark kaleidoscope behind her eyelids. A sense of well-being unfolds inside her, stretching its limbs. Even with her eyes closed everything is beautiful.

She hears a bird singing and opens her eyes to look for it, which is how she sees the white people coming out of the woods. She crouches down so fast she almost falls on her onions and doesn't have to look again to know that most of them are polices. They're heading toward the market, but their words come back to her on a wintery wind: "clearance" and "timeline" and, most alarmingly, "shit or get off the pot."

She sits for a while after they're gone. Finally she raises herself to the windowsill again, and there's the robin, obviously suprised to see her. He flies away, which is wise because even though she loves robins, she can't help but wonder how they taste.

School

When she was little she lived with her grandmother, Alouette. They lived in an apartment building: not a project like Kidland across the swamp, but an old stone building with THE WYLOCK. carved over the door. It's a long way from here—probably a hundred miles, she thinks. The street was called Clatchy Avenue.

Her grandmother was very smart. Reka wants to be that smart someday, which is why she keeps up with her studies although certain people at court think she's wasting her time. Alouette was a teacher before the polices came, and after they closed the schools she taught Reka and sometimes other children at home. She did other things too, like sewing and writing things down for people and baking (Reka doesn't like to think about the baking). And many, many years ago, before all this happened, she took care of Reka's mother, who was a little dickens with her hair in braids. Reka would love to have braids again. She's tried to imagine herself with them, but it doesn't work, probably because she's no longer sure exactly what she looks like. Sometimes she remembers Cesario and wonders if one of the girls in his house knew how to braid hair, and if she would have braided Reka's.

The fire is banked, the tarp drawn closed and secured with rocks. The ladies are embroidering or painting tiny pictures on pieces of ivory. She opens the Traveler's book and finds today's lesson:

> But to return to my anomalous position in King
> Arthur's Kingdom. Here I was, a giant among pig-
> mies, a man among children, a master intelligence

> *among intellectual moles: by all rational measure-*
> *ment the one and only actually great man in that*
> *whole British world; and yet there and then, just as*
> *in the remote England of my birth-time, the sheep-*
> *witted earl who could claim long descent from a*
> *King's leman, acquired at second-hand from the*
> *slums of London, was a better man than I was.*

"Do you understand?" she asks Vanessa, the only lady who shows an interest. As Queen she used to have her own tutor, a fluctuating figure now brusque, now kind. But lately she finds she is more interested in teaching other people. Vanessa doesn't know the word "anomalous," so Reka tells her to look it up. "Where?" Vanessa says.

"In the dictionary."

"What's a dictionary?" Vanessa says. Really, these people are just too ignorant. How do they get to court in the first place? She takes it out and shows Vanessa how to find the word. "Write it out ten times," she says, noticing a definition futher down the page. Vanessa says she has no paper. Exasperated, the Queen puts a stick in her hand and points to the ground.

> **an•o•mic** *adj. Socially unstable, alienated, and dis-*
> *organized.* —**anomic** *n. A socially unstable, alien-*
> *ated person.*

That makes her feel strange. She doesn't appreciate the things the dictionary says to her sometimes. To distract herself she looks up "alien." There is a long entry and then she looks up "extrinsic" to see if it is related to "extra" but, as usual, the little recipe at the end explains nothing at all.

> *Latin extrinsecus, from outside: exter, outside; see*
> EXTERIOR + *-im, adv. suff.* + *secus, alongside;*
> *see* **sek (w-1)** *in Appendix,*

which she doesn't bother to do, knowing from past experience that there's no point. Her own uselessness overpowers her. She puts her head down on her knees, and nothing anybody says can persuade her to raise it again.

She sleeps restlessly and wakes up angry. Why does she have to live like this, surrounded by trouble? Why didn't the Traveler take her along? She's just a little kid. And she's unbelievably hungry. Reka knows she isn't growing properly, but even so there's a hole inside her that starts around her lungs and seems to reach down to her toes, and no matter how much time she spends gathering food she can't fill it up. She'll check her turtle trap. She used to think she wouldn't eat a turtle, because of their scared little eyes. But actually the problem with turtles isn't that you feel sorry for them. It's that you have to whack them with a big stone more times than you have breath for, and their scaly legs go on jerking and twitching even after you start hacking them up, which she personally is so bad at that most of the meat just disappears. Also, you never have enough water for soup, so you have to roast whatever turtle chunks you've managed to save, and they taste like old tire. And when it's over you're still hungry.

She lies there staring at her pitty wall. The side of the overpass is deeply pocked and pitted, and that's where she has arranged her treasures, one in each little hollow. She has bones, stones, feathers and sticks, including one burl of wood she thinks is quite remarkable; also three shells (one pearly inside), several buttons, a shard of purple glass, nine sequins all different colors, a gold coin with ONE FARE on it (not real gold or she would have had to sell it long ago), the remains of a crystal necklace she found on the tracks, and a whole pile of cubical green diamonds from a car window. Sometimes she gives little tours of the museum. "You don't see many of these around anymore," she will say of the green diamonds. Or, "Our preservation department washed this feather in rosewater to preserve it." She doesn't want to give a tour today. Who's listening anyway? She'd like someone to explain something to her for a change. And if she can't have that she'd like to read a book. A new book, with pictures on the cover and a plastic wrapping.

A while ago, when she was living somewhere else, she found a library. It was called the North Harbor Free Public Library Poland Hill Branch, and it had bits of colored tile stuck to the outside, which turned into a picture of children cartwheeling if you stood far enough away. The floor was covered with shattered glass and trampled paper, empty bottles and chicken bones and a few dead rats. That was where she got The Three Musketeers and Die N-Word Die, also I Know The Caged Bird Sings and two mold-spattered cloth-covered books called On The Sublime French Revolution and Treats Of Cicero And Pliny. She took them home and put them with the other books she'd collected, and a couple of months later her whole nest was flooded with stinky black water and every single book was ruined, except the Traveler's gift and the dictionary, which were in her bag at the time.

She got to read all of them first, though. She didn't like the bird book or the one about treats, and she didn't like N-Word either, although the person who wrote it said some good things. For instance, he said a major problem for black children is authority, which Reka knows is another word for polices. This is true, because polices go into your house, and also polices have guns. The reason she didn't like his book was he put down school. Reka has never been to school, but she knows it's in a building, probably heated, and you get lunch. They probably even let you sleep there. And she's also heard, though she doesn't quite believe this, that they give you books.

With all this in mind she arrives at the old high school. Here's another thing she wouldn't do on a good day—cross the swamp so close to Kidland, where smart people do not go, to stare at a flat-faced stone building with windows in regiments across its front. In the middle a wide fan of steps leads up to an enormous doorway, twice as tall as Reka, but instead of a door there is a solid wall of concrete. She climbs the steps and inspects it, fascinated by the incongruity of a wall where a door should be. Did they fill the whole building with concrete? She imagines a flood like the one that destroyed her books, only gray and heavy, creeping through the corridors, overtaking students and engulfing them, pouring sluggishly over trophies knocked from shelves.

When she turns to go there are three boys at the foot of the steps, gazing up at her. One has a golf club and they are all wearing denim jackets. They look interested, which is bad.

"What you doing, shorty?" the golfer says to her. "Tryna go to class?"

She backs up against the door which is not one. There is no way to evade them, unless she dashes left and leaps off the top step. But the drop is blocked by a rusted handrail, and the muddy ground would suck off her shoes. She can't go right, because a fourth kid has come around that side of the school. "Who the fuck is this?" he says. He has a gold nose-ring hanging out of his nose, and the beginnings of a beard.

"Don't know."

"She was here when we got here."

He looks her over. "What's this?" he says, tapping his own chest and pointing to the water filter, which she has forgotten to tuck under her clothes. She would like to do that now but can't lift her hand.

"She don't talk."

"She retarded."

"Ugly motherfucker, too."

"Yo, Royal, we need bitches."

"I wouldn't fuck no ugly, retarded motherfucker. Shit."

"You all shut the fuck up." Suddenly Royal's face looms at her: he has grasped the railing on his side of the stairs and pulled himself up. His breath comes at her thick with cigarette smell. He has one foot up on the rail and he's reaching for her water filter, saying yo let me see that one sec. Finally she can move her hands, and she bats him off until he gets two fingers around her wrist and pulls hard. Her stomach convulses, hot pee shoots down her legs, and the world goes upside-down and hits her in the face. "Aw man!" voices say. "That's disgusting, yo." Voices fade. She lies head below heels. Some piece of her skull hurts like you wouldn't think a bone would hurt. Time passes.

Closet

The sky is almost dark. It is not blue and not purple and looks transparent but isn't. Her first thought is what a lovely color it would make for Vanessa's ermine gown. Her second is to wonder where the smell is coming from. Confidentially, her personal physician kneels down.

"Sir Mordred," he says, "worked some dark magic here."

One of the ladies bursts into tears. The pain in the Queen's head slops around like liquid in a bowl. Her attendants bring emollients and softest lace, and soothing oils are spread on her cheekbone. In a moment of panic she grabs at her water filter—no, it's there.

"Can you walk?" Hazel asks her.

She can walk. She takes the remaining steps slowly. Hazel offers her arm, and they proceed towards the trees, the worried, wailing ladies, the physician, and a small pageboy running to lift the Queen's train from the mud. "We will seek no revenge," she says without turning around. "The Traveler forbids it."

"What if the Traveler's wrong?" says the little boy's voice behind her. Hazel wheels about, threatens to have him whipped. "Shut up, Hazel," the Queen says, and then she must spend the next ten minutes soothing the lady's feelings. People think life is easy for a queen.

They make their way over the bridge. It is dark now, and with the darkness has come a pelting rain. Everything is equally dangerous at night so she takes the road. She hurries, head down, one wrenched leg aching, glad to be near her boiled-root supper. Then she gets home. She can't see the tarp; it must have blown down. She fumbles in her bag, holding it close to keep the rain out. Her long-guarded box of matches is almost empty. Lighting the broken candle, now she sees. The tarp is gone. In that sheltered little corner between two slabs of concrete—not underneath the bridge but outside, against its flank—there is no mulchy bed, no quilt of newspaper, no cooking pot. What used to be the firepit is a hill of mud, dancing in the rain. The perfect gentle slope of earth where she studied has been gouged away. Her treasures have been raked down from the pitty wall and trampled, the shells crushed to powder, the smooth bones snapped. She stoops over the mess, holding the candle together by its middle. She sees some of her green diamonds, but the smell rises before she touches them. They are smeared with shit. She is standing in it. A red message is painted on the wall. The message says:

SHOUDA WENT.

"Aah-aah-ahh," she says, a tiny moan that comes out of her mouth involuntarily. The boys from Kidland—how did they get here before her? It's happening again. Dread draws down like a thick curtain, enveloping her until she can't see forward or backward and all she knows is the depth of her wrongdoing and the certainty of punishment. She howls, scaring herself. Where can she hide? She turns and runs, stumbling as she tries to scuff the shit off her shoes. Her mouth is open, panting, and her throat is making whimpering and wheezing noises like a puppy. She trips over a rock, crashes face-down into the mud, gets up, collides with a tree. One leg is sending rays of hurt into her bottom and up her back. She just keeps running until the hurt goes away. All she can do is run. She can't stay anywhere, she can't be safe, she can't have a home or a grandmother or a bed, but she can run.

She dreams about the ladies. Not her own ladies, whom she will never see again, but the ladies in the apartment house, the ones who came after her grandmother was taken away.

She is on the top shelf in the closet. She can reach it from the stack of boxes if she jumps high and grabs, and Alouette always makes her go there when the polices come. People don't look up, Alouette says, and Reka has found this to be true: even if they do open the closet, they don't notice her. Alouette always knows. She knew that Reka wanted cupcakes for her birthday, and she made them even though they're not allowed.

But Alouette isn't here now. The polices busted in the door and said something about illegal commerce and Alouette was gone before the smell of cupcakes left the apartment, and the last thing she said was you'll be all right sweet baby and when they asked who she was talking to she said, the dog. Reka has been up here in the closet ever since. She doesn't know how to get down. She can get up but getting down is scary and Alouette always helps her after the polices go away. And now here come the ladies. She knows what they're supposed to say—they say it every time. That Alouette is one stuck-up black bitch. Think she special. Always did like this red teapot. You sure we cool? Hell, she ain't coming back. But today something is wrong. They've found Reka. They must have come through the ceiling, because they're looking down at her. And not saying what they're supposed to say. What they say is:

You have got to be fucking kidding me.

I'm serious, Owen.

What do we say to Skip? Sorry, we can't come back to civilization yet, we just found our model sleeping in a pool of her own piss?

We take her with us.

Are you insane?

Do the shoot at Coyson. What do we have a studio for? Clean her up, do the test shots tomorrow, client approval on Saturday night.

She's young.

That's compelling. Better than a crackhead, anyway.

Either you're a mad genius or I'm about to lose my job.

Could be both.

Could be.

The Traveler

It must have been night, because the ladies went away and everything was very quiet. Then she was awake again, heart slamming against her chest. "You gonna tell the Brothers?" a new voice said.

"Hell no. You know they just be grabbing it for a secret headquarters or some shit."

"So what then?"

"We move in our own damn selves."

"What if she comes back?"

"I told you. Don't nobody walk out of a Processing Center."

"I mean the other one. Reka."

"Oh, her. She can come back any time."

"Yeah?"

"Anytime she want my boot so far up her ass she fly out that window."

She was afraid to jump down from the shelf. She thought she might break her bones or even die. Still, she managed. Seeing her room in daylight made her feel better at first, then worse. She emptied the books out of her carrybag and put in Orange Dog and her pajamas. Then she put in two of the books she had taken out (A Wrinkle in Time and Roll of Thunder, Hear My Cry) and went into the kitchen. She packed bread and crackers and some apples and a flashlight. After hesitating for a second she also took a steak knife. She took some money out of the coffee can. She locked the door behind her.

For a day or two she was half-convinced that Alouette would appear and smack her for leaving the building— the avenue—the neighborhood, until the dimensions of her malfeasance grew too large to comprehend. She met people who gave her food and sometimes bottled water, and who laughed or frowned when she asked how to get to the Processing Center. Some kids knocked her down and stole her bag, but she ran after them, screaming, until they dropped it. The next night a man let her stay in his car. His fat fingers stuck her where it hurt, and she had to jab the knife into him before he opened the door and let her go.

Things weren't so good after that. She stopped walking where people were and kept to the empty places: alleys and parking lots, the blind backs of old factories, side roads strewn with garbage. There were rocks and pieces of concrete piled everywhere, rearing higher than her head, with twisted bits of metal sticking out like claws. There were chunks of bricks, dirty mattresses, old tires, chain-link fence sagging from broken poles. She didn't see a single intact building—roofs were caved in or windows were shattered or a whole front was missing and gobs of wiring dripped from exposed floors. Helicopters flew low over the road, battering her with noise. She was very thirsty. She heard shots; she knew they were gunshots because each one stopped her heart. Then it started to rain.

She had always loved the rain. Now she understood that that was because she didn't know what it really was. It was an eyeless, loveless, punishing thing, bent on demolition and ruin. It ate away human works, and what it couldn't eat it flattened, and what it couldn't flatten it transformed. She saw it topple a traffic light, sending the heavy head crashing to the street. It turned her coat into a bag of water and her bag into a soaked pulp and her shoes to nothing. It smelled like sick things and toilets. And it kept coming on, burrowing endlessly into the ground, bringing the whole world down with it.

She lay curled up under a sheet of corrugated metal beside an immense scrap heap. The badness in her stomach was unbearable. Sometimes when it crested she was able to crawl outside a little ways and poo, but other times she was too tired to move or nothing came out. Her head hurt, and she could feel how hot her face was without even touching it. Things became very strange, so that she had to ask herself seriously whether she was awake or asleep: the metal tentacles sticking out of the scrap heap came reaching for her; the neighbor ladies gathered and said, "Look at that raggedy-ass hair." The junkyard flooded in a torrent of rainwater that carried her and Orange Dog for miles, hurtling them backward over the broken landscape to the Wylock, surging up the stairs and through the apartment door, and Alouette was angry about the mess. She woke up as dazed and bruised as if she really had been to Clatchy Avenue. The ground tilted and swung, and she tried to hold on. Everything fell away except her own name, and she knew if that slipped away too she would die. So she said: Reka. Reka. Reka.

"Hello?" A darkness blocked the light. "Someone in there?"

Reka fainted again. After a long time she had concluded that she was fainting and then unfainting, over and over. That was what she did mostly. When she woke up a person was among the tentacles with her, gathering her with difficulty into their arms.

"Orange Dog!" she cried. They said, "Fuck me."

Thin soup in a scratched plastic cup.

"Where's Orange Dog?"

"Orange Dog couldn't come."

"Is he on the rain?"

"The train?"

"The rain. Rain."

"Yes," they said, "he's on the rain. Having a nice ride."

"When he come back?"

"That ride only goes one way, hon. It's a one-way rain."

"This is a place for you to get well."

Reka wasn't stupid. She knew it was a school bus.

"Who are you?"

"Just a traveler," the person said.

"Are you a nurse?"

"No, baby."

"You look like one." Reka didn't know why she had said that. She, the Traveler, was not much fatter than Reka herself, with a pointy face and a big, loose natural. When she smiled, her mouth went down instead of up.

"You're a girl, right?"

"Yes, I'm a girl," the Traveler said. The smile came, but it was different now. The muscles around it moved differently. More material for Reka's special project, the study of the Traveler's smile. Her grandmother always gave her lots of projects. She said, "Can we draw?"

"Draw?" said the Traveler, who sometimes seemed not to understand what was said to her. But she traveled away the next morning and came back with some pieces of paper and broken crayons, as well as more soup for Reka and a can of beans for herself. They drew animals, which Reka was good at, and pictures of the Wylock. The Traveler said it was important to remember the street you came from, even if it made you feel bad. You could organize around a street. Organize what, Reka asked, and the Traveler said, "Resistance."

"What's resistance?"

"It's when people stand up for their rights, to be treated with dignity and respect."

"Do you know where the Processing Center is?"

"Don't ever go into one of those," the Traveler said. "Those are bad places, you understand? Don't go into the city, ever." Her voice was loud and hard, and Reka started to cry. She could not control her tears, which always came very suddenly and outside her will, and she hated herself for that—for being little and soggy and without dignity. This time, though, the Traveler held her. Reka laid her head against her breastbone and heard her own scuffling breath. "It's okay," the Traveler said. "Just watch out, be smart, you'll be okay."

As Reka got stronger, they went for walks. The bus stood crookedly in a field overgrown with prickles, dandelions and clover. When Reka was tired, the Traveler carried her on her shoulders. She walked up and down the field with her, keeping Reka's ankles in a firm grip. Up and down, up and down in the bright morning sun and in the golden-colored evening. They looked for butterflies. They sang church songs, like "I've Got a Testimony" and "Can't Nobody Do Me Like Jesus." Sometimes Reka rested her head in the Traveler's wild hair and, putting arms around her neck, fell into a jostling sleep. She woke in the school bus, often knowing right away that the other was traveling, and wondering if she would ever come back. When the Traveler was around she watched her like a hawk, like two hawks, one for each eye.

The Traveler was a teacher, too. They read a book about King Arthur that she found in the city, and even though Reka didn't know all the words, the Traveler explained things to her. They started to draw pictures of the Yankee and Sandy. It's good to read a little every day, the Traveler said, especially if you're sad. It's okay to be sad, you know, she said. We all have feelings. She said, it's important to try to love other people. Don't ever hit anyone. Don't hate anyone. And try very, very hard to love yourself, because you are infinitely precious. But Reka knew it wasn't true, because if she really were, the Traveler wouldn't leave.

She came back one night with a bag full of things. One by one she laid them out on the floor. Matches, twine, toilet paper, soap, seed packets—these are easy, she said, you plant these in the winter and these ones in the spring. These ones are zucchini, you'll have so much zucchini you'll wish you never laid eyes on a zucchini seed—check it out, a sewing kit.

And this, this is very important, Reka. This is a water filter. Look, sweetheart, you put this part in the water, and you pump to clean it. It travels through the filter and ends up in this little cup. She put it on a piece of twine and tied it around Reka's neck. Don't ever drink water without pumping it first. The water here isn't clean, that's why you got sick. Promise me.

"Don't leave me, please! Don't leave me!"

Snot ran down her face. The Traveler wiped it off with her sleeve. She said, I have to go.

"I won't love you if you leave me. I'll hate you. I'll hate you forever."

The Traveler looked tired. She said, it doesn't matter about me.

Boot

She's been away such a long time. For a while she was on the ocean, or so it felt—rocked and flung in squalls of wind and noise, her eyes blinded by electrical storms. Then she was alone in a dark close space like a coffin and voices were shouting outside. She was onstage, which happens sometimes in nightmares. Hands moved over her skin and painted her mouth and nose with liquid plastic. Bad things took place.

Now she is here: a smallish room with beige walls and no windows. There is a desk, a chair, a bed that she is lying on. The sheets are smooth, the desktop gleams; everything is smooth-smooth and beige. The air feels warm and thick, like there are too many ingredients in it, and tastes as sweet as candy. She badly needs to pee. She struggles to sit up against the frictionless sheets and lowers her feet to the floor. Then she tries to stand and almost falls over as the carpet seems to move like live fur under her heels. She must proceed very slowly to what she hopes is the bathroom door.

It's like a heart attack! As soon as she steps in, light blasts every surface in the room. She looks down at the agonizingly white tiles and sees her black foot slide forward. Step by squinting step she finds the toilet. While she's seated she closes her eyes, but the light still hurts. She wipes off, hops down, and eases open one eyelid until she can see a big silver button, which she presses. The noise is incredible.

When her eyes are less afraid, she checks out the mirror. There's her face, same as the last time she saw it. Is it, though? Has she always had that crooked bottom lip? Or those things that look like cuts beneath her eyes? Suddenly she understands: she is being processed. This is the Processing Center, and all that noise and light, the paint on her skin and the organizing of her limbs—it's all part of the process of turning her into someone else. The idea is so terrifying that she clutches the sides of the sink and a column of clear water shoots into the basin and splashes her in the face. She flails backward, trying to slap the contaminant from her skin, and falls across the threshold. The bathroom lights go out.

Her own shaky breathing fills her ears. She is twisted, with one hip down and one up and her cheek to the carpet, and she feels twisted inside too. Why did she come out this way, all crabbed and unlucky? Maybe they'll process her into a straighter person. Over her fear, like wind stirring grass on a hilltop, sweeps a current of rage. They better not! She never said they could do that to her. They never asked!

She's gasping, and she knows that's not good. When you huff and puff people can hear you, but when you breathe slow and regular, like this, they walk right by. Gradually her breath fits into its accustomed tracks. She turns over on her back and stares at the top of the door frame. It looks like an upside-down wall. If a race of tiny people lived on the bathroom ceiling, they'd have to climb over it to get to the bedroom. She used to discuss that with her grandmother, she remembers. She lay on the floor while Alouette was sewing and considered how ceiling people would think the hanging lamp was an enormous tree. Now she listens to her breathing. How does it know how to go in and out like that? It keeps your heart beating, Alouette said once. My heart, she thinks, my very own heart. Nobody else has the same one. All at once she has a sense of herself—her intrinsic presence. She is a girl who lies on her back thinking about her heart. What did the Traveler say? Infinitely precious. She wonders if it could be true.

Her sleep is harrowed by noises too loud to hear and light too bright to see. Cesario has put her on a box. "Just look right here," he says. "Look at me. Perfect. Unbelievably perfect." No, it isn't Cesario but a white man. He's the one processing her. His name is Edmark. "Hold still, love. Let me take a look … That nose has to come off. Anyone have a sharp pen? No," he says, "Skip, believe me. These flats are going to get everyone's attention."

She's lying on the bed, covered in sweat that feels like glue, listening to his voice.

"It's not like they didn't know what they were getting. They signed off on the concept."

Another white man's voice rumbles. Edmark says, "It's risky, of course it is."

"We have the focus groups to back us up," a hard voice says.

They're on the other side of the door that doesn't open. She thinks there are three of them—too many to run from if they come for her. The one with the hard voice says, "… hypes as well as jumbos."

"I'm opposed to hypes," Edmark says.

"Your opposition is noted."

"The power of this image is the stillness. The stillness and the scale."

"Get China to tap over the second test shot. If they sign off, we can roll on Tuesday."

"Monday night."

"Whatever."

"I'm going to go see her," says Edmark.

She slips silently off the bed and squirms beneath it. The carpet has no smell. Its fibers scratch her face. She lies absolutely still. There is a burst of laughter from the room beyond. She wishes she had her bag. Her grandmother's knife is dull now, but last winter she got a box cutter in exchange for a broken watch face and two batteries. Though she's afraid of blood, and of hurting people, it would be good to have a piece of metal in her hand.

The door opens. His voice says dubiously, "Love?" Other voices retreat behind him. "Yeah, fuck you too," he says.

His footsteps. "I brought your dinner, love." A sound she hasn't heard in a long time: the clink of dishes. "Chicken Mirabile, Rubyleaf Salad, fresh-baked Rollovers and a completely out of this world Hazelnut Tarteline. You'll think you died and went to heaven, believe me." She can see his cowboy boots, covered in some kind of reptile skin. They rock back and forth for an indecisive instant, and then he squats down. Not low enough to see her—and she sees only his big denim knees—but low enough for a hand to descend and roll something towards her. It stops an inch from her face, just before she would have jerked away and hit her head on the bottom of the mattress. It smells like bread.

The chair scrapes on the floor. She hears the drumming of his fingers on the desktop.

"Well, it's on," he says. "China's tapping over the work we did yesterday. Assuming client approval, in two weeks your face will be all over the city."

She has no idea what he means by this, but it still makes her feel sick.

"You're doing an outstanding job. Don't let anyone tell you different. Your eyes alone are worth every fucking dollar in the budget." He starts rapping the desk with his knuckles. She tries not to flinch with each report. "Excuse me, sorry. You don't curse, do you? Of course not, you don't talk. I just mean you seem like the type of girl who doesn't curse."

The rapping suddenly stops, leaving a silence broken only by the uneasy sound of his weight shifting on the chair. She's so tense her bones may crack if he stays much longer. "Listen," he says, "I know this hasn't been—it's been disruptive. I can understand why you might be a little upset. But this really is the best thing for you. At least you're out of that shithole, right?"

What surges up her spine isn't fear. She grabs the roll and hurls it, with a hoarse cry, right at his crocodile toe.

House-broken

Waking out of a deep sleep—for she does sleep well, now that she has them at bay, though her days are anxious—she is instantly alert. Somebody's trying to open the door. She can hear the rattling. Someone is coming to get her, and for no reason she thinks of Royal, the Kidlander captain with the gold ring in his nose. Though she's frightened of Kidlanders, she will join them and wear a denim jacket and do whatever Royal says, just as long as he takes her home. But seconds pass without incident, and she realizes the sound she heard was not rescue but the machine that controls the air in this place, switching to another setting. No one is coming for her. She is stuck here, and while she is no longer afraid they are going to rub her out, to erase the presence that is Reka, she is at the same time even more miserable because she has to endure this as herself, alone.

She has questions. But they are not as important, right now, as not giving anybody any answers. Whatever it is they want to do with her face, Reka will not let them. If they want her in the studio, she has to be carried there. When they try to stand her up she goes limp. If they want to take a picture she closes her eyes, and if they keep trying she screws up a horrible expression and sticks out her tongue. Once when she did this she heard people in the back of the room laughing. Edmark is frantic.

"Look, No Name," he says to her, "we contracted with these people for a five-week roll-out. That means at least twenty separate brand images. I thought we were working well together? I thought we understood each other."

Owen comes in and says in his hard voice, "That one

understands bite and kick. That's all."

"No Name, honey. Do you want me never to work in popshow again? Edmark Whitman the third," says Edmark, "so young, so full of promise?"

"I told you, take the food away. Then she'll be on your box quick enough."

She can't stop eating, it's true. She is growing fat on chicken and hazelnut tarteline. She has also decided, after close observation, that everybody here uses the tap water, so now she washes several times a day. Edmark says no, they can't starve her. She's a juvenile in their care. "There must be laws," he says.

"You weren't so worried about laws when we took her out of SAPID."

"We were desperate! Two weeks of casting without a single face! Anyway," he says, "you can't argue with that first flat."

It took Reka a while to figure out what a flat is. Edmark kept showing her the little plastic box he carries, which has a screen like a TV; she could make out parts of her face on the screen but didn't know what the other stuff was. Tiny cars, figurines, a model railroad village? When she realized he was showing her pictures of billboards, like the ones at home that are usually falling down and losing their messages, her whole body got hot. She felt like crying, but instead she screamed as loud as she could. She started jumping up and down and screaming, wagging her head like a crazy person, until he ran out of the room.

"So pull up some outtakes, tap them into new backgrounds and throw the little beast back."

"Listen to yourself," says Edmark. "Are you seriously suggesting I use our discards to fake up the rest of the campaign?"

"This business is not about artistic integrity, Edmark."

"I deny that. I deny it absolutely."

"Enjoy your denial," Owen says. "Because when Skip gets back from Australia, he is going to fire every son of a bitch on this account."

After Edmark leaves he says to her: "Let me tell you

something too real for Edmark's tender ears."

He pulls the chair up to the bed. He is a tall man, where the other is short; brutal like a police, where the other is fussy and forgetfully kind. "There's a name for people like you," he says. "All you poor extra fucks on the other side of the wall. You're called non-qualified. Do you know what non-qualified means?" She has an idea. "It means you have no identity," Owen says. "You're not on the payroll in any factory, you're not registered in any township. You don't exist. Which means we can do whatever we want with you. Me and Edmark and the people who pay our salaries. And do you know who those people are? I'm taking you through this step by step."

She glares.

"The people who pay us are the executives of Coyson Stone. And who pays them? Without getting into technicalities, those people are paid by the capital market. Who controls the capital market? The government. And who controls the government?" He waits, raising eyebrows on his stone-white forehead. "You don't know, do you? You're not as smart as you think you are." He gets up. "Let's just say they're people who are very, very interested in this campaign. And they're not about to let a stupid little cunt like you stand in their way."

She wants to disappear, back into the rocking darkness and the ocean, but she can't. It should be like falling asleep, and now that she's so full of hatred she feels like she'll never sleep again. She can see Edmark doesn't like it. He tells Owen that the energy is wrong, and Owen says Edmark is getting his flats, isn't he?

She hates him so much. The knowledge that he sat there and said those things makes her want to stick her fingers in his face and rip it off. She wants to paint things in his blood. The hatred howls through her at night. It's like a flooded river that joins the river of her fright to become a torrent. She can't eat. She doesn't want to wash. She can't summon up her ladies or even remember what her nest looked like. Edmark is worried. One of the studio people comes and offers her a purple-colored fruit, but she just turns away. A doctor comes and says she is withdrawn. But Edmark is getting his flats.

Some nights she thinks she'll be good. Edmark said something about twenty pictures. If he gets them all, won't they let her go home? But the truth is she's not completely stupid. Ugly, maybe, but not stupid enough to believe they'll send her home once this is over. The world just doesn't work that way, in her experience. If she ever does get home she's going to learn to fight, and if the Traveler doesn't like it, the Traveler can lump it. Just as she thinks this she misses them with all the force of both rivers raging inside her—the Traveler and Alouette and Orange Dog and even Hazel and Daffodil, although they're not real, and the dirty creek with its robins and the great green leaves of knotweed along its banks. And the dried tendrils of an old grape plant still intricately coiled through a broken chain-link fence. She saw a bullfrog once: a black lump of a thing with translucent, delicate hands. The inside of its mouth was bright pink. She hasn't seen the sky since she got here. She will never forgive Owen for that.

She begins to pay more attention to the studio people. They are all fresh-looking and have straight shining hair. They don't have bruises or scars, and their white skin is smooth like marble. There is one brown-skinned man who sits in front of a big television screen. When pictures of Reka slide onto the screen he touches them all over, changing things. Between shots (unless Edmark turns around and screams at them to shut the F up) the studio people spend a lot of time laughing. Life is just one big joke to them, apparently. And though she gathers that they're all on the job, none of them seems especially glad to be employed. They joke about Skip Stone and his assistant, China, a tall girl in tight skirts and high shoes who looked Reka over and said, "At least it's house-broken." They can say whatever they want about China, as far as Reka is concerned.

All of them, she finds, carry those little plastic boxes. The boxes are studied, touched, spoken to and held to the ear as if they were telephones; based on this behavior, Reka decides that they are walkie-talkies which also show pictures.

Everything belonging to these people is named. Names are printed all over their clothes and possessions, even hairbrushes and tissues, and of course their walkie-talkies. Every day, the first thing they do is crowd around the food—the quantity of food in the studio is mind-boggling, there's an entire table covered with nothing but bread—and look at each other's names and comment on them. Oh, you have the new Hensbane? Let me see your Work Ethic. What are those shoes? Cordelia Fine, can you believe it? Did you catch the hype last night? That was one of mine. "Children!" Edmark has to yell. "We come to make popshow, not to praise it!" Popshow is their name for TV.

At first she thought she was very far from home. Increasingly, though, she doubts that. From what she can remember of the journey with Edmark and Owen it didn't take much time, and they were in a car, not a plane. Also, every now and then someone mentions the place she came from. They don't use the names she knows, like East Woods or Poland Hill; they say "the other side" or "over there." She hears them say Edmark's a madman. Could have gotten himself killed over there, they say. It's a failed state. They don't want peace. You know we build schools over there, and those people just tear them down. They can't get to us so they kill each other. I heard there are bodies rotting in the streets.

"Maybe we shouldn't ... ?" someone says. It's the girl who tried to give her the purple fruit. The others look at Reka and she stares back. She wants to tell them they are stupid wrong losers. They don't know the first thing about the place she comes from if they think it has streets.

"Stop worrying, Jenny, she can't understand English."

"Maybe Ebonics," says somebody else, and they laugh.

If Royal the Kidlander ever shows up here, not that there's any reason to think he would, she doesn't know why her mind is stuck on him, he's sticky somehow—if Royal shows up she'll have some questions for him. She'll ask him why people here think everything is so funny. And she'll ask about the food. If there's so darn much of it that Edmark's team can't eat it all, and she sees this every morning and afternoon, why don't they give the leftovers to people on Reka's side? If they're afraid to go in, they could just throw it over the wall. The people on Reka's side would eat scraps off the ground, no problem. Reka herself once sucked on dirt after spilling water on it. Reka was once so hungry she tried to eat a slug, and it took her two days to stop retching.

She lies awake in a maelstrom of questions. Yesterday she saw the light-skinned man outside the bathrooms. In a low voice he said, "Hey, how's it going?" He's a careful-looking guy. She has seen him smiling and laughing with the others, but he's careful inside. "You hanging in there?"

Only because he was brown, she gave him a chin jerk. The names covering his shirt were so tiny they looked like lace. "You're doing great," he said, and quickly touched her on the shoulder. She wondered if, if they caught him speaking to her, they would put him up on Edmark's box instead. "After this—you'll see, you can write your own ticket." He bent closer. "You have to remember the work goes out into the world," he said, almost whispering now. "It reaches more people than you or I could ever reach in person."

The world? Were they planting pictures of her on the shores of—Appalachia? And he thought that was a good thing? If she were still queen, she would have his hands cut off. She turned away and walked into the bathroom. But now, in the middle of the night, he troubles her thoughts. He made an effort; he wanted to tell her everything would be okay. How can he not see that nothing is going to be okay again, that her life is almost over? Why is he blind to the truth in front of his nice, smart face? And if a black man thinks her salvation lies in billboards, what hope is there for Reka?

☞

The little hallway where he spoke to her is a good place to hide. It's where she waits for Jenny.

"Oh—No Name!" Jenny says. "You scared me."

She holds out her hand, points at Jenny's plastic box, holds out her hand again. "Can you talk?" Jenny says.

Reka snaps her fingers, points. She wiggles all her fingers. Edmark will call out for her any time now. "This?" says Jenny. She looks around. Then she puts the box in Reka's hand. She watches for a moment and then says, hesitantly, "You know how to use it, right?"

Reka turns it over and around. It is red and patterned with pink flowers, except for the front side or face, which is a silky-looking grey-green surface that darkens where she touches it. There are no buttons. She pokes the screen as she has seen them do, and pictures race across it as Jenny murmurs, "No ... no, you see—" She pokes faster, stabbing the screen. Her finger leaves little craters which seem to fill up with green liquid that turns back into pictures. Images are blooming and dying all over the screen, jumping like raindrops in a river. "No, honey, let me show you." Reka turns her back on Jenny. In desperation she shakes the box and is badly scared when it opens like a book, scattering an assortment of instruments—makeup brush, bracelet, a piece of chalk. With a yelp Jenny goes down on her knees, and Reka hurls the box over her head, where it cracks with a loud sound against the bathroom door, and bursts into tears.

People arrive, saying "What the hell?" and "Jesus, is that your tap?" But Jenny has abandoned her instruments. She has come and put her arms around Reka, who sobs like an infant, like somebody with the right to cry.

III

AN HOUR IN THORNS

1

Dear Cay,

Everything is fine, fine, fine. I am fine. Bucket 13 is fine. Hiding all the time is fine. Eating ten beans for dinner is fine. Having no money because I can't get a job because I'm not work-qualified because you can't get work-qualified until you have a job is fine. Spitting on the ground after the police walks away because I can't do anything else is fine. God everything is so fucking fine out here and I miss you. I miss your beautiful dick my Cay. I wish I had it here so I could hold it tight when I got cold and shove it up myself when things get so bad that even gem won't help, though what passes for gem here is nothing you want up your nose or mine. These sorry bastards be snorting salt because it put them in <u>mind</u> of gem, I mean it is some serious ghetto up in here and I am a snooty light-skinneded bitch, thank you very much.

I met a girl. You know I love you and your dick. You know I think about you day and night even though you wouldn't come with me, you dick, so don't be mad okay, I'm not a lesbian but I met this girl. You didn't tell me Cay how delicious pussy is. I mean you said it was nice but I never knew it is so spicy and slick and juicy and when I have my face in it I forget how fine everything is and I only want to eat her sweet pussy until she screams. She's twenty. She has a rash on her face from the air in the factory and her eyes have permanent red spots. Her hands are so cracked she has to wear gloves or else she might get some of that dry crusty stuff inside

her hands onto the components. I watch her kids all
day then she comes home, if she gets to come home,
and we you know what. But I'm not supposed to be
here because I'm not work-qualified so we can't go
outside, and her neighbors don't like me and they
don't want their kids to play with NeNe and Jason,
and they don't share food. Janelle gets paid once a
month and we have three weeks to go.

Love,

me

She folded the pages up in eighths, sixteenths, and then
with difficulty into thirty-secondths. She wrapped the packet
in some metal wire and inscribed on an exposed corner:

WALL TOWNS
FREESIA STREET
CAY JACKSON

"Where's the drop?" she asked the girl beside her.

"Huh?" said the girl, waking. Sleep took Janelle whenever
most of her body was on the bed. Lore had not mentioned
to Cay (because it embarrassed her) her fascination with
the girl's meaty breasts.

"The drop. Where I can mail this."

"I don't know."

"Come on, you know—the mail drop. Don't you ever
send mail?"

She shook her head and flopped over on her side. "What
about your family?" Lore said. Janelle's parents lived in the
interior, where they worked a small illegal farm, but her brothers and cousins were in Bucket Nine. "Don't you write to
them?"

She turned and looked at Lore out of her sleep, her
round forehead screwed up against the baleful touch of
the waking world. Just before she fell back she mumbled,
"Don't have nothing to say."

After she left for her shift in the morning, Lore tidied
the kids up (they slept in their clothes, having only one set

each) and took them over to Miss Mindy's. Miss Mindy was short and solidly packed and ran a day-care out of her shack. She looked at Lore over the bent stub of a cigarette. "What you want?"

"I'm Lore? I'm staying with Janelle."

"I know who you be."

"I wonder if you could watch the babies for like an hour?"

"Why?" She exhaled towards Lore's ear. From behind her came a desperate-sounding wail. "I thought that was your job, snitch."

"I'm not a snitch."

"Watch the kids while she feed you information on what we doing here. Ain't that how it go?"

"Look, I'm just asking you to watch the children for an hour. I can pay you."

"With what, bitch?" Her heart-shaped face was taut with dislike. "Some of your town money? I don't need no help from you. You want to drop Janelle's kids here? You tell her she come down and pay like everybody else do. One man, one day."

"What?" Lore had seen a lot of bad shit over the past six months, but this took the fucking cake. "You're pimping out these women for childcare?"

"You want to go to the police?" Miss Mindy squared herself in the doorway, planting her feet apart and crossing her arms. " 'Oh, Mister Police, they a woman in the shacks who so bad! She so mean, she call me names!' You think they give a fuck? I been arrested ten times. You know what happens if you go to the police? They love them some yellow ass. And when you get home, that shit shack of Janelle's done burned to the ground."

Lore started backing away, bumping the children along behind her. "You're evil!" she yelled.

"You're a middle-class informant bitch!"

She was shaking. She hurried Jason and NeNe back to Janelle's hut and took down the rest of the beans. "You keep your sister in here," she told Jason, "and don't go out. You understand? Here's lunch. Don't go outside that door, or I will whip you." Jason's large, oval eyes took her in from his wary little face.

She cried as she walked to the center. She had starved on the dirt roads of the interior and in factory yards. She had slept in a crevice between two slabs of concrete, hiding herself from the spotlights and shotguns of the police; she had been carded by men as human as a pair of stainless-steel shears, men who told her she wasn't qualified to eat or work or stand on this patch of bare ground. But she had never been threatened by another black woman, and she thought her heart, already as dry as Janelle's ruined hands, would crack open and leave her dying here in the farthest corner of the world, below the hills that marked the edge of Bucket Thirteen.

The center of the factory cluster was completely paved over. It was a cement square, about half a mile to the side, scoured with winds or scorched by the sun. Cement security kiosks rose at intervals; the rest of the surface was covered with vendors' carts and lean-tos and other semi-legal structures, with crates of junk and portable stoves and people selling forms or travel applications and families huddled in blankets. At midnight the police came out and swept everyone off the plaza. Lore didn't know where the families went then, but she had passed by such places in the dark, and she knew they crawled with other, quieter forms of commerce from which a single traveler did best to keep away.

Now someone came up to her and said, "You want ID?"

She said, "Mail drop." She couldn't see the guy—he was behind her left shoulder. "What do you think this is, the towns?" he said, and was gone.

What the hell was so difficult about a mail drop? She was sick of this bucket and its ratty, skittish, beaten people who wouldn't lift a hand to help themselves. Janelle was no different. When they first met Lore had tried to reason with her, but you couldn't reason with someone who worked twelve hours a day on a production line. She worked to feed and shelter her children, while the roof leaked and the kids grew thin on lettuce and macaroni.

Lore pushed on through the square, shouldering past hustlers, laborers and drunks. Her anger was galvanic but also milky, a thick, cooling concoction of whitish-green that spread through her and calmed the brain twitching in her skull. How sweet if she could express it, fill the square with it—drown them all in the viscous aloe of her rage!

"ID, ID, ID. Work paper, form help. ID, form help, work paper, form help. ID ID."

She turned to see a burly character with a tattooed neck. He looked down at her and said, "Form help thirteen, thirteen form help. Work paper twenty to fifty, ID two hundred, two hundred bucks."

"Mail drop."

"Go back to the towns."

"Wait." She caught his shirt. "Where are the Brothers?"

"Fuck you, snitch."

"Wait." Lore opened up her face to him. It was something she'd learned to do on the road. People in the buckets had faces that funneled downward, into scowls of hate or fear; a raised, open face, she had found, could not help but give them pause. "I'm not a snitch. My Uncle Tony, he's with them."

"What his name?"

"Anthony Maxwell."

He pulled his shirt from her fingers. "I'll tell him I saw you."

She stood alone on the cement, cursing herself. Fifteen minutes later, as she looked for a way out, thinking of Jason, something went right through the middle of her head.

She was tied up. That took a long time to understand. She was lying face-down on a scratched wood floor. Her arms were pinned up behind her back, pulling tendons in her shoulders and neck into spokes of frightening, cramped pain. Her cheekbone was pressed against the floor, and she could hear the tight rasp of her own breathing. Something heavy chipped against her jaw, words were shouted, and the heavy piece struck her again. She wasn't afraid of a bullet cleaving her flesh, but of the barrel, so cold and ridged, crunching into her jaw and causing her more pain. She was terribly afraid.

"Where you from? Where you from, bitch?"

"The towns!" she said, groaning it out against the foul-smelling floor, although the words tore her aching tendons. "The wall towns, eastside!"

"Then what the fuck you doing here?"

"Are you the Brothers?"

A shod foot came down on her head. Not with a crash, but with a slow, grinding weight that turned the bones in her head against her. This is how it's done, she realized. How the body is destroyed. So fast.

"Answer the questions, then we discuss that," a new voice said, and she loved him. She loved him, he had said "then"; he had saved her life.

"You just hoofin' it? This whole way, you walk?"

"I got some rides." Her body felt rawly empty, as though her skin were mere casing. "Farmers. Even some Brothers."

"I was not aware of that," said the guy in charge. He was a hulking man, six-six at least, with hollow forward shoulders and a bald head.

"Terrence mentioned it," said another man. "Brothers be picking up hitchers in the stretch, he said."

"Have you been in the stretch?" the leader asked her.

She nodded.

"How is it?"

"Worse than here," said Lore. She had forgotten until just now. The memory of what had happened to her in that wild country made her feel for her pocket and bring out the letter to Cay. Dispassionately the man said: "We don't do mail. As every fucker from here to the hills done told you, I have no doubt."

"But why?"

He rose, still holding the gun, and took the nugget of wire-bound paper from her hand. "Because, Loreen, every Brother is a dead man," he said. "And the dead don't have no need for letters."

If she wanted to join them, she had to become dead as well. "We can do that one of two ways," he said. "We put one bullet in a revolver, hold it up to your head and pull the trigger. Or, seeing as you so young, we can make a exception and just pull a train on you."

She looked around. There were four other men in the room—two cleaning guns, one coiling the nylon rope that had been used to hold her, and one just standing by the door listening. Some disturbance in plane had affected the doorman's face, setting one eye lower than the other. He showed neither excitement nor dismay at the idea of repeatedly raping the spirit out of her.

"This is how you fight for freedom?" she said.

"What'll it be, Loreen?"

Her hands and feet were numb. She felt as though she might detach from them and float up to the ceiling, an unmoored trunk, severed by grief from the rest of the human race.

"I'm not going to die here with you."

"You die in here and join us, or we kill you out there."

"I'm not going to die here with you!"

The man in the doorway caught her by the neck. "I'm not dying, you rapist motherfuckers!" she screamed. "There are women and children wasting away in those fucking shacks, you trigger-happy pieces of shit! Why don't you take your big hard dicks and go down there and shoot some fucking police? I'm gonna kill you. I will kill you, rapist pigs!"

"Take that fucking whore outside and blow her head off."

"Don't fucking touch me—*oh*!"

They were outside, behind a wall of buildings. The tilt-eyed man jerked her backwards, wrenching her shoulder out of its socket. He turned her toward the horizon.

"Run."

2

The hills were not what she expected. She learned later that that was part of the strategy behind SAPID: it was a geographically discrete place, full of natural internal divisions like mountains and rivers that served to isolate inhabitants from the rest of the country and from each other. People like her, who had walked the length of it, were rare; most stayed in their clusters, or moved from one bucket to another along the transport highways, or kept to themselves, like Janelle's parents, on a tiny square of earth without knowing what lay beyond.

In Thirteen, people spoke of the hills as a savage place, filled with police who shot on sight to defend the import processing zone which started at SAPID's borders. They said it had been devastated in the bombings twenty years before and was populated with robbers and fanatics. In fact, once she had painfully and very slowly scaled the steep rocks that rose above the bucket, she found herself on a street not unlike the one she grew up on. It was a broken street, and she was used to that too.

Later she knew it as Maquette Street, but there were, of course, no signs. It wound along the cliff edge, from which it was separated by stretches of patched fencing and runs of uneven green yard studded with small, bent trees. Here and there a large oak tree which had survived the bombing served as a gathering-place; though she saw no people, kitchen chairs were placed under the trees, sometimes a desk or a tent. On the other side of the street, the surviving houses were large and looked much-repaired: some were half-covered in plywood that had been painted with murals. A few shacks had been put up in the empty spots where there were no houses, and somehow—this was one thing they'd always had trouble with on Freesia Street— the rubble had been carted away.

The street was overwhelmingly green. In the bucket, she'd forgotten it was summer. The sun was going down, turning to deep blue the leaves that crowned the saplings and hung in swags from the old trees and filling the weedy lawns with shadow. There were wildflowers and wisteria spilling across the yards, ivy climbing the fences. It seemed like years since she had seen a neighborhood so full of growth. She wanted to lie down in the weeds and let the ivy cover her until she stopped breathing.

Where the street turned away from the cliff there was a barricade, and a police checked her ID. The old insult of being corralled like an animal seemed to find no place in her tonight. It circled, unable to settle, as the police scanned her travel permissions, and she thought it would leap out and hit him. The police took the card out of his reader and gave it back to her, and she walked on.

People began to pass her in the near-dark, going the other way. The road dwindled to a meander of dirt between two barren fields. More people came, some of them carrying what looked like grocery bags. The only time Lore had ever seen a grocery store was in a place called Fort Hock, where hundreds of police lived with their families. There had been armed guards posted outside the store to keep black people from coming in. Hunger jabbed under her ribs. She began to think of hurling herself at one of the bag-carriers, knocking them to the ground so she could get at their supplies. She was small and knew she was agile and fast. What held her back was a fear purer and more commanding than any she had felt before, even in the stretch. It was the fear of her own extinction, and it hung on her so heavily that she broke into a sweat; her feet slowed, then stopped, and she stood in terror of her life on an empty road.

"You almost there—just the next house up."

The person who had spoken to her moved on. But Lore was incapable of motion. She found herself squatting on the road, then prone on it, shivering against the pebbles. She put her arms around her knees and hid her head as best she could and lay sick at heart, waiting for the strike.

In the morning she was still alive.

She got up and went on to the house. It stood alone at the end of the street, an old triple-decker with the top missing. A girl was sitting on the porch smoking.

"You okay, hon?" she said.

"What?"

"They said there was someone in the street, and you didn't want to be touched."

"I don't remember," Lore said.

"Have a seat." She rose as Lore climbed the splintered steps. "How about coffee?"

"Do you have ... food?"

"All the surplus is gone, hon. But you can have some of mine."

She came back ten minutes later, holding a green plastic plate with bread and jam on it and a glass jar steamed up with coffee. She put them down, unwrapping the scrap of towel she'd used to hold the jar. "Kamal, brush your teeth!" she yelled back into the house. Lore could hear other people inside. "You go on," the girl said. She was short and big-chested, with long dreads down to the middle of her back, black-rimmed glasses, and freckled skin drawn tight over broad cheekbones. "I need to get some stuff done." She went back inside.

The sun, the jam, the empty road with its wheat-colored, tasseled weeds. Lore sipped coffee from the jar—it was half-chicory. She wished she had her letter to Cay. *Dear Cay, I am eating jam. Not as good as Auntie's, but good.* How had she let them go so long without news of her? Alice and Ira must think she was dead. What had seemed an imperative breaking away was revealed in the morning light as a shitty, childish thing to do to her parents' oldest friends. She fumbled with the laces on her sneaker and pulled it off. Turning it upside-down, she probed the eroded sole for the folded piece of paper she had wedged there. It was moldered into a pulpy gray triangle with velvet edges, but she took a broken pencil from her pocket and began to write: *Dear Ira and Alice. I am so ...*

In black parka, sunglasses, and canvas work pants, a police was coming up the road. She placed the evidence in her lap, as plain as the sun flashing on his glasses.

"ID please," he said. But he didn't put it through his reader. "Henry, six oh six three oh?"

"My name is Lore Henry," she said.

"Scanned you last night." The ID hung in his hand. He wanted her to reach for it. If she had seen a single scissors in six months, she would have shredded that motherfucker. "I never forget a non-Q."

"My name is Lore Henry," she said again, aware that her voice was rising. He smiled, and the ID dropped. She could not stop her eyes from following as it cut through the air and landed in the dirt at the foot of the porch steps. She forced them up again. His face was brutally amiable, with a prominent square frontal bone. He looked like someone well-satisfied with his contribution to society. His boot lifted, moved over the card. She did nothing. He'll split it in half, she thought, then arrest me for being undocumented. I'm about to go to prison. The boot descended and scuffed backward, hard, and the card went flying.

"What's that you've got there?" he inquired.

She wouldn't go easily, she knew. That was her fate: if he reached toward her, she would start spitting and howling and get her skull cracked and be dragged off for hard processing. She wished she had stayed with the Brothers, where you only had to die a little to be free.

"Can I help you, Supervisor Merriman?" said the dreadlocked girl, opening the door.

He looked up. "Food night last night."

"I'm sorry, Supervisor. We don't have any surplus here."

"I'm sorry you're sorry, Casey," he said. "Because I sure would like some biscuits. And some collard greens—you got some of them?"

Casey came out onto the porch. She was dressed in a

pair of overalls that had lost their metal hardware; the straps were sewn onto the bib. Her feet were bare and her dreads had been gathered back into a ponytail. "I'm afraid we don't have collard greens," she replied. She sounded no different than when she had greeted Lore an hour ago. "We'll be happy to fill a list for you, though. All you have to do is drop it off here by seven P.M. next Tuesday."

"I'm not here for that bullshit," said the police, sounding markedly less collected than Casey. "I'm not a fucking co-op Negro, you understand? Give me what you have or I'll shut you fuckers down."

"I can't stop you from helping yourself. But please be aware that I have an eight-year-old boy inside, as well as a number of people who worked all week to bring that food in yesterday."

"Get out of my fucking way."

Casey sat down next to Lore. Once he was in the house, she gave a very small sigh.

"Is your son going to be all right?"

"Oh, people will share out the rest," she said.

"I mean—"

"Merriman won't hurt anyone. He just wants to make a point."

He barged out, holding bags of cheese and cuts of meat and several apples that dropped and rolled away. "Next time, half the share in a bag. Down on the road so I don't have to come into your stinking pigsty," he said. And he marched off, not at all unhappy-looking from the back. Casey stared after him, knitting her eyebrows behind her worn-down glasses frames.

"Obvious question?" said Lore.

"Why don't we join forces and keep him from taking our shit?" Casey said. She turned to Lore and smiled. "Welcome to Middle Hill."

3

She dreamed every night of traveling back to Freesia Street. Unspeakable things happened to her in her dreams—everything she had survived since winter and worse. When after interminable journeys she reached her home, nothing and no one remained to greet her except the corpses of her parents, hideously decayed, and Merriman standing over them, eating an apple. At meals her stomach was like a bowl of bile. She had a dull persistent ache in her head, and spikes of hot white-gold glittered at the periphery of her vision. Sometimes these barbed constellations moved to the center of her view, and then, try as she might to twist and turn her head, she couldn't see the price list she was working on.

"Go on up, I got it," Casey said.

Doggedly she kept writing. "Get the heck out of here." But she could not see the stairs. "Deshawn!"

Deshawn was three or four years older than Lore, lanky and stooped. His eyes were protuberant as knobs in his set, uncompromising face. On Sunday nights he handed out vegetables in complete silence. He helped her upstairs without speaking, but when she turned towards Kamal's room he said, "You can use mine."

She fell down on the bed and said, "I'm not fucking you."

"I don't want to fuck your blind ass."

Lore pressed her fingers against her eyeballs, setting off explosions of vitreous spikes. "Quit that," Deshawn said. "You making it worse."

He seemed to have squatted down in a corner of the room. She closed her eyes. The clusters danced frenetically, as though lashing out against their own dissolution.

Then, one by one, they faded.

"You don't go to no meetings."

She opened an eye. He was still there in the corner, big hands hanging between his knees. His skin was dull, almost powdered-looking. He wore the denim pants and shirt of a Kidlander, but they were ragged and full of holes.

"Why should I?"

He didn't answer. "I've been to meetings," she said. "Plenty of them. People get together in a room, they argue, they make a chart. And shit just goes on the way it was."

"That how it be, huh?"

The endless wash and break of adult voices in the night. Cigarettes in the hallway, boysenberry wine. Ira with his gray-stained beard laughing like nobody's business. "Yes, that's how it be."

Deshawn got up. "I guess you right," he said. At the door, without looking back, he observed, "Not so fucking smart as they say."

"What?" Lore said. But he was gone.

Hatred, anger, and grief were her occupiers. She was their scorched playground. And in the center of the blight burned a small, wavering sense of loss, for she knew she had once been capable of happiness, and it hurt her more than anything else to think that that part of Loreen Henry was dead.

Yet she remained her parents' daughter. The hill-dwellers were the only people she'd met who were actively working to improve black lives, and as fucked-up a creature as she had become—as dearly as she wished to pass her life moldering beneath a twist of sheet—that meant something to her.

"This is our new sister, Lore Henry. Her parents were peace activists in the wall towns."

Although her mother was very far from that she said nothing. Deshawn was there, also saying nothing, as well as Casey in her coveralls, a tall turbaned beauty named Nafula, a Haitian-looking girl and some others. Russ was Brother Chair.

"The work of the Organizing Committee is popular

education, decolonialization, institution-building and strategy. First agenda item, communication. Sister Latesha?"

A young girl with slanted eyes and oily black curls rose to report. No luck repairing the radio transmitter. Also, most streets lost their receivers in the raid. Brother Mattie had a electronics textbook and would bring it to the communications working group next Tuesday. Meanwhile, the girl suggested they focus on the newsletter. Maybe Sister Lore, who did such a good job on the price list, could help with it?

"Where is Brother Mattie?" asked Brother Chair.

"He suppose to be here, I don't know."

"Okay, good report. You two sisters can get together after the meeting. Sister Nafula?"

She didn't stand up because she didn't have to: her very nose—winged and slender—commanded attention. The nonviolent curriculum was in place on Kilhasset Avenue, and she was meeting with the Education Committee next week to discuss wider adoption. Could the sister go over that curriculum one more time, she was asked, for members who might have missed the last meeting due to a previous commitment? Would the chair be referring to Brother Ricky? He would. In that case, could Sister Nafula inquire, as a point of order, whether chasing tail constituted a previous commitment?

"Oh, you going there, Nafula? Is you jealous?"

"Boy, you know Nafula she way over your grade," said the Haitian sister.

"Yeah, you still in kindergarten and she a post-doc," somebody else said. Another contributed, "She have *bigger* ambitions."

"Did I miss anything?" A man entered the kitchen. He had a bald head and a limp, and the sight of him made Lore's throat close up. She glanced at Deshawn, slumped in his chair with his eyes half-lidded.

"Brother Mattie, you're late."

"Again."

Lore stood up. "Why is there a white man here?"

"Brother Mattie's not a white man," said Latesha.

"Holy shit," said Brother Mattie. He checked out the back of his hand. "I'm cured!"

"Asshole, obviously you white. I just saying you ain't a *white man*."

"Excuse me!" Lore said. They all looked at her, and their united gaze only made her feel more crazy and upset. "What is he doing here?"

"Brother Mattie is on the committee," Brother Chair said.

"I won't work with a white person."

Hold on, sister, they said. Keep it cool.

"Look at him!" She pointed, and it felt like the whole of the last six months was shooting down her arm. "Don't you know what white people do? They murder our families. They enslave us in factories and steal the fruits of our labor. They take food from the mouths of our starving children. I've seen it. Haven't you? Hasn't everyone in this room spent every day of their lives learning what white people can do? We live in a hell of the white man's devising. Y'all can pretend that's okay, but it's not okay with me!"

"You, ah, you want to address that, Brother Mattie?" said the chair.

"I'm not addressing him. He best not address me," Lore said. But the white man answered pleasantly: "With all due respect, I think the sister is overgeneralizing."

"Motherfucker!" She grabbed a stoneware mug and let fly at his head.

The flurry was like a crowd of pigeons taking off, the voices like the roar of an engine. Plus Brother Chair saying: "Okay, Sister Lore, outside."

Alone with her in the hall, he had the weighty, ruminative manner of men she'd grown up around. Those diligent thinkers of a demolished world—how measured they were in their proposals, how majestic their hopes. She felt so tenderly for their misconceptions she could hardly stand it.

"That all you got? Or do we need to hide the knives?"

"You think any white man be hanging here for love?" She was on the verge of tears. "How many of y'all's meetings has he already reported to SAPIDAD?"

"Let me ask you something, Sister Lore. Do you always

get up on a soapbox and preach to your elders?"

"If my elders is damn fools it ain't no fault of mine."

"Mattie Foster came over in a boxcar, just like the rest of us. You the fool if you think we don't know who real and who ain't."

She said sullenly, "I'll quit the committee."

Russ leaned against the wall and adjusted the highly smudged glasses that were too small for his wide, good-natured face. A lot of adults in Middle Hill wore spectacles, she'd noticed. She didn't know if that was because they had better medical supplies than other populations or just worse eyesight. "I think you better not."

"What are you talking about?"

"I'm talking about you getting your act together so you can be of service to this community, instead of spreading your darkness over hill and dale as you been doing."

She would fucking show him darkness. If that's what he wanted, he had it.

"You like Middle Hill?"

She shrugged.

"You want to stay?"

"Where else can I go?"

"Then do something for me. For the next ten days, in your head, Middle Hill is Opposite Land. Okay?"

He wanted her to conjure up the opposite of everything she felt. "When fear and anger come into your heart, call up forgiveness and love. When you hate someone, just open your mouth and say to them, 'I love you.' Even if evil white Mattie come chasing after you with a sledgeham-mer, I want you to stop and turn around and just open your arms."

"Wait a second," Lore said. There were people dying all over the territory. The Authority was free to kidnap and execute anyone who got in its way. Blacks had no rights, no civil liberties, no legal representation and no organized means of resistance. "And you want me to spend the next ten days telling people I hate that I love them?"

The man whom a year later she would see shot like a dog looked out Casey's back window and smiled. "It's a beautiful day out there, Sister Lore," he said. "Why don't you go get some sun?"

The kitchen table was covered with scraps of paper—work credits for her to transfer into a ratty ledger that must have been fifty years old. Casey said, "That was my only mug."

At midnight she went up and knocked on Deshawn's door. Hearing nothing, she opened it. He was lying on his bare mattress in the middle of the empty room, hands folded on his ribs between the open flaps of his shirt, looking at the ceiling. He glanced over. "Gonna throw a mug at me?"

"Ha ha," Lore said. She came in and pushed the door closed. The room was large; she wondered why no one else was sharing it. He was motionless, staring upward, even when she sat down on the bed. His torso was hard with muscle on a rack of bone. His nipples, widely set, were half-covered by the shirt. The laced hands were as big and dusty-looking as the rest of him.

"You like it here?" she asked.

He shrugged against the mattress ticking.

"Why do you stay?"

"Can't leave," he said. "Caps kill me."

"What's a cap?"

"Captain."

"Every cap everywhere has been told to kill you?"

He shrugged again. "Ain't worth testin'."

"So you don't want to die?" said Lore.

Deep within his eye socket, one lid twitched. "What you want?"

She swung a leg over and straddled him. His cock rose instantly against the crotch of her jeans. He kissed greedily, big teeth clicking against hers, with one hand gripping her side over her left hip. "Fuck me blind now," she said in his ear. She ground down suddenly and felt him almost come between her thighs. "Blind as all y'all."

Okay, she was spoiled. Janelle gave what she got, and Cay was almost thirty. It wasn't like that with Deshawn.

"Motherfucker, it ain't difficult. Just turn around and lick what you find."

"Nah, that's okay."

"No, it ain't. It's not okay, Deshawn!" She was livid and ashamed. He'd made it so clear that cunt wasn't something he would sully his face with. "You know what you are? Trash. You're just a piece of gangbanging trash."

A tiny line appeared between his eyebrows. He seemed to consider, and his bulging eyes—the only mobile part of his face—moved restlessly around the room. "Look, where I come from, women is bitches. Shorties or bitches. That's all." He paused after this lengthy declaration, then added in a faintly pleading tone, "It ain't personal."

She rolled as far from him as possible. Presently curiosity got the better of her, and she said, "What's the difference between a shorty and a bitch?"

"A shorty, she keep things clean, you know. Cook and do the wash and shit. A bitch be for, uh—"

"Yeah, okay," Lore said. "And what about you?"

"What?"

"What are you for?"

He came up in a blood click. Blood, he said, was like enforcement. You made sure the dogs, the foot soldiers in other clicks, behaved; you cleared the way for product distribution. He'd killed his first man when he was eight, raped his first woman when he was ten. Plenty of other work for a blood dog, too. Ain't never no reason to take the day off.

A raw, sickening revulsion spread through her like nausea, and the spikes flared in her eye. Brother Russ, she thought, you better help me now. She raised herself on an elbow above Deshawn lying naked as a corpse and summoned love. It came in a flood, like a long-penned dog surging out and leaping on its owner, like a downpouring of summer rain. She thought, holy shit.

"SAPIDAD! Open the fuck up!"

She had time to get a blanket around herself. They

wouldn't let Deshawn dress. They marched him out of the house and made him kneel, hands behind his head, in the center of a loose semicircle of people—Maquette Street people and others, holding children and huddling together. A car pulled up and shone its headlights on him. Police in yellow reflective jackets moved among the crowd. She could hear the murmur of protest and the short, harsh answers: "ID please. Registration number. Qualification status." Some people fumbled in their pockets, trying to be helpful. Others were struck dumb by panic, and the police shone lights in their faces and shouted their demands.

"You cock-sucking scumbag. I should process you right now."

There was an oval of light around Deshawn, and Merriman wove through it, holding his gun. No, she thought, this is not going to happen, not when I made love rain down on someone for the very first time. Please, God, don't take your blessing from me now. Don't scorch my heart until there's nothing left. And then she knew there was nothing left. There was no God, no blessing, no salvation. All she had was the rain.

4

She liked a dark man. Hakim said she had a reverse paper-bag test.

"Have you ever slept with someone as light as you?"

"No," she admitted. "But you just saying that cause you jealous of Deshawn."

This brought guffaws from around the table. "Enough, enough!" said Sister Chair. "We have a revolution to build, people."

"If I can go back to what Sister Tammy said, I think it would be insane to send Mattie. No offense, Brother Mattie."

"None taken."

"It's shooting ourselves in the foot," Phillip continued. "I'm all for equality, but we have to be realistic. People will ask why we chose a white man to represent us."

"We can paint him brown," Lore said.

"Sister." The chair did not appreciate her sense of humor.

"It will destroy our credibility. I can't believe we're even talking about it."

"I think we should trust the people," Lore said. "Let's not assume they can't understand that white people are a part of this too."

"Like how you understood when you threw a mug at him?"

"Am I ever going to hear the end of that mug?"

"No, Lore, because it's exactly what you'll be dealing with if you go on the road with Mattie."

Latesha said, "We missing the point. It ain't about what other people think of us, it's what we think of ourselves."

"It very much is what other people think of us, sister," said Nafula, the chair. "Half of organizing is P.R."

"But I'm saying, how can we represent love and harmony to the people, if we don't have love and harmony for ourselves?"

"I'm the one going on the road," Lore said. "And I want Mattie."

She knew that Russ and Nafula and Phillip, the most experienced members of the committee, disapproved of her conduct in meetings. "You bully, you don't process," Russ had said to her last week. Now Hakim had his own issues. He thought she'd brought up last year's liaison with Deshawn in order to put him in his place, which was only partially true. Deshawn knew her game—she firmly believed he deserved better from the people of Middle Hill—and told her to drop it. He still lived alone in the big room in Casey's house, sorting food orders and building furniture to earn his work credits.

"They treat you like shit."

"They afraid."

"Well, they should see that I'm not afraid."

"You go ahead," Deshawn said. "Save the world with one hand like you do. Other hand down somebody pants."

These were the comrades she truly loved: Casey, whose evenhanded goodness benefited every lost creature in her path; Russ, who stilled the bawling kid in her; little Latesha, who'd lived fifteen years under white rule without losing her sweetness; Margaret from Michigan Avenue, who had been fighting for justice long before she was slowed by Enclosure and emphysema. They were the teachers and companions from whom she daily learned the art of letting pain, grief, impatience, depression, vengefulness, antipathy and frustration dissolve into air. But Mattie was a crazy motherfucker. Mattie was her friend.

"I was down in the bucket last night," he said, handing her a joint.

"What's in this?"

"I got it off Johnson on Pekoe Street."

She sniffed suspiciously. "You mean Salty Johnson?"

"Not so salty," Mattie said and winked.

He was a man of middle height who shaved the graying fuzz from his skull every week and had a three-inch scar, perfectly perpendicular to the earth, running down his left cheek. His smile was missing two teeth, one on either side. He was a horndog and a reprobate, a cheerful nihilist who committed filthy acts in factory urinals and came back in the morning to tend his vegetable garden.

"I saw your sweetie."

"You did? Did you tell her about coming up here?" It would definitely complicate things with Hakim if Janelle moved onto the Hill. But wasn't it time to complicate things with Hakim? Blindsiding him with Deshawn had gained her just the briefest of respites from his muscular devotion.

"I barely got to talk to her. It took me ten minutes to convince her I wasn't police and her break is only eleven minutes long."

"Isn't that obscene? You know how many hours she works a day? In a rush, fifteen to nineteen. You know how she got that job at Factory Five? She had to go stand in line every day for ten days. When she finally got in the door, they gave her a test that lasted four hours, and then she had to get a gynecological exam. Can you believe that shit? And she doesn't get any treatment for environmental hazards. Her hands are like Death Valley, Mattie."

"Lore, baby."

"What?"

"NeNe is dead."

She had died of malnutrition. Janelle had taken a day off to bury her and had been fired from Factory Five. She had paid the rest of her month's food to Miss Mindy for a clean ID and was working illegally at Factory 22A, terrified of being discovered and blacklisted. Tears rolled down Lore's face. "Oh, God," she said, "oh, poor NeNe, oh God."

"I'm sorry, love."

"I should have stayed with them."

"Yeah, you could have stayed." Mattie scratched the crude tattoo of barbed wire on his white arm. "And you'd probably be dead by now."

"I could have saved NeNe."

"And fifty just like her would die just the same."

She despised him for a second. Of course he didn't give a shit about a black baby. Her whole body was clenched up like a muscle. It was peristalsis: the involuntary movements of her hatred, trying to expel what she had learned. She tried to relax but her frightened body would not permit it. Let go, let go! she thought, and it came in and surrounded her. This was nonviolence, then—wave after wave of loss, experienced without defense. Not just her own pain, but Mattie's for his lost lovers and missing family, Janelle's for the child who had starved to death, NeNe's own confusion dwindling down to dazedness and the dark. It all rolled over her, and again she thought, there is nothing else.

News came to Middle Hill in tiny, tightly knotted bundles. This town was starting a food co-op; this village wanted advice on digging wells. Ministers wrote of crowded churches and too many funerals. Lore and a companion would travel to these places and others, working to link them in a coalition that could spread across the territory. "You are seeding," Nafula said. "And the seedpod is a very simple and very powerful organism. We use it in our study groups. The first three classes teach the basics of nonviolent direct action, and the last one teaches you how to seed another group. You'll be using exactly the same method."

"What if they don't want to learn?"

"You get out of there and move on."

"Your movements are going to be visible," Phillip said. "If you get a chance to radio, SAPIDAD will hear."

"Could I have a gun?"

"She isn't ready."

"Sister Lore, you understand that if you don't live these principles, you won't be able to teach them."

"Give me time," she said, pissed off that she was being asked to carry their message into the desert and believe in it too.

"We gave you plenty," said Brother Russ.

Her co-educator would be Casey, who was bringing Kamal along. Kamal was a quiet nine-year-old with his mother's large eyes and a habit of reading any scrap of print he could get his hands on. He was by far the smartest kid in Lore's schoolroom, and the nicest, too. Lore didn't understand.

"You should be protecting him."

"You think so?"

"Yes, for God's sake. What if something happens to him?"

"What if something happens to me?"

"Exactly. You should stay home. Everyone who has ties here should stay home, and I should go. And maybe Deshawn," she added hopefully.

"Oh, no, we need him here," Casey said.

"Who?"

"Deshawn is a great teacher of peace. Haven't you noticed?"

Rapist, murderer, drug soldier. Yes, she had noticed, but she'd thought she was the only one. Deshawn's presence in the town was like a hole torn in a green hill. To live with him, you had to learn the paradox of forgiveness.

She was happy. Love had returned to her life, she had children under her care, the elm trees on Maquette were dark with foliage and the smell of wood shavings filled Casey's house every morning. And so she was leaving. Sorrow no longer rent her heart, she believed, but filled it with something golden—tears spreading like honey in the blood.

The raid came as expected. On the night before the educators were to leave, a hundred people were rousted from their beds and hauled into the overgrown lot between Parnay and Dutchess Avenues. Lights on stilts were erected and glared down on the crowd. Police with flat voices directed them to move up, move up, make room, step together. More and more people were brought and squeezed into the lot. Lore could feel the elbows and backsides of her neighbors pressing against her. "Now, people!" she heard Merriman yell out.

They all knew Merriman wasn't dangerous. Although he was verbally abusive, and he hated them, some glitch in his training or long-forgotten idiosyncrasy of his upbringing prevented him from inflicting real violence. But there was something different about him tonight. Everyone felt it and everyone was frightened, with the deep, convulsive, dehumanizing fear that has no antidote.

"Now I have put up with your bullshit long enough! You have broken the law, you have defied the government, you have stolen things that don't belong to you! This town is a nest of corruption and insurgency! But now I hear you're taking your act on the road. I won't fucking stand for that, people! Who's responsible? Who's going to take this cesspool of a town and spread its filth all over the Interim District? Fucking answer me!"

Casey's voice said, "You know who we are, Supervisor."

"Smith? Where's Henry? Where's that fucking non-qualified vagrant?"

The crowd around her began to scrape away, motion by tiny motion. She realized they were helpfully giving her room to step forward. "Damn, y'all want me killed?" she muttered. She got to the front of the lot and saw that Merriman was not alone. Another police, in military uniform, was standing beside him. They shared some words, and then the military police came up to Lore and Casey. "Are you both travel-qualified?" he asked.

He was smaller than Merriman, and the lights gave him a sallow, almost green-tinted face. Lore felt instantly that there was nothing negotiable about him. He didn't like his job, and he didn't dislike it. He fulfilled his responsibilities. He eradicated dissent.

They showed their IDs. "They're legal," he said, without turning his head towards Merriman. "There's nothing we can do."

"Sir, these people are scum. They'll attack infrastructure—they'll do anything."

He addressed the crowd. "You have a former gangster here." Nobody moved. He stepped back, surveyed them, and pointed to Deshawn. "You." He snapped his fingers, indicating a place in the light. Deshawn walked into it. He faced the military man, slightly slouched, his hands engaging each other briefly before parting to fall at his sides. "You are a criminal wanted by the Administration of this District. You have been tried in absentia and found guilty of death-penalty acts under Title V of the Qualified Enfranchisement Act. I will suspend the penalty if these two women remain in the precinct."

He answered very softly; no one beyond the front row of people could have heard him. "That be up to them."

Lore felt Casey's hand seeking hers and squeezing it hard. At the same time, she saw, Casey was pushing Kamal behind her. Quietly their neighbors closed ranks around him, and the same minute pulsations moved him backwards and out of sight. All over the lot, children were being swallowed up and moved backwards by the crowd.

The military man turned to them. Casey's hand was like a vise. "What do you want to do, ladies?" Lore looked at Deshawn and found him looking at her. She didn't know what was happening inside his head, but afterwards she was glad that the moment had come to pass, the moment of their recognizing each other's humanity and being together for the last time.

5

The mud was cold and slimy on their faces. The community plots were set up in ragged rows beneath ancient trees which come summer would shield them from view. Even now, in late winter, the interlocking bare branches of elms and willows hindered surveillance and added to the confusion of brown and gray detritus—pine cones and fir needles, shattered tree limbs, sprung fences and rusted wire gates—that made the garden look abandoned. The three of them were lying full-length under a pile of branches that must have been gathered for their defensive properties: they were covered in thorns, some short and fringe-like, others as long and hard as tapestry needles. One of the latter pierced the back of Lore's calf. Casey lay with one arm around Kamal, pressing him into her body. Lore's head was turned toward him and she could see his starkly thin, alert face. At the beginning of the journey he had wanted to keep up his schooling, and they had read the contraband copy of *Beloved* by firelight. Then one day he told her he'd had enough. The book was not for kids, he said. It made him too sad.

She whispered to his mother, "I'll distract them."

"No," Casey hissed. The hand that had been around Kamal's hip shot out and gripped her by the wrist. They lay still with their arms joined above the child. There was a violent rasp of nearby radio static. "Uhh, what's the description on those women?"

The police was very close. They could hear him fumbling for his transmitter and clicking it on. "They're two black women with a child. What the fuck else do you want?"

"That really narrows it down, Patrol," the static said.

She was trembling into the mud. The mud was a mold and she was the gelatin. A twig cracked not three feet from her hand. She had never felt so keenly the power white people had over her body. The police was retreating. "Two black bitches with attitude," he was saying. "It's not rocket science."

"The kid have an attitude too, Patrol?"

"Fuck you, Dispatch."

Even when he was gone, they didn't move. The patrols who came after them were men both cunning and bored. They had often waited a long time to exercise their full force, and they gave enthusiastic chase with shrieking sirens that nearly paralyzed Kamal and dogs that turned Lore into a whimpering child. They shouted threats Lore wished she had never heard and took delight in predicting what would happen to all of them in prison. What these patrols also did was pretend to leave and then double back, so Lore and Kamal and Casey lay under the branches for about an hour. An hour in thorns was very long.

Their destination was Millrock, a council in the eastern stretch which served as a kind of communications hub—it had both a mimeograph machine and a radio tower. But that night, after Kamal was asleep, Casey said to her: "It's time."

They held each other in their coats stuffed with leaves. They had no sexual relationship, but Lore knew every scratch on Casey's skin. "Yes, you should go," she said.

"I don't want to."

"It's the right thing to do."

"I thought it was right to bring him." She wept, and Lore locked an arm around her bowed head and kissed the tears on her cheek. "Look what I've done to him."

"It was." She gathered and arranged Casey's dreads, remembering the first cup of coffee in its steamed-up jar. The sunlight from that morning on the porch lingered, despite the deaths of Russ and Deshawn, despite the hurting inside her and the soil and struggle of their lives now. "Things change."

"I love you so much," Casey said. In the morning she and

her son turned west, and Lore went on to Millrock.

In March she visited a village that had no name. It was surrounded by a high cement wall, and the plan was for her to climb the wall and jump down into waiting arms. But the villagers dropped her, and she broke her knee. Lore laughed so hard she almost didn't feel the pain.

Her hosts were Fantom and Marie. Marie was a big woman with a burned face and a wide orange bracelet made from part of a traffic cone. Fantom was a writer who had tagged the outer wall by hanging upside-down from its top while a chain of people held onto his feet. They had to get creative, he explained, because they'd been inside for fifteen months. "Before, we did actions in the factories. We had sing-alongs and dancing, right on the factory floor. So they built the wall to keep our extreme dopeness contained."

"How do you get food?"

"They truck it in. Occasionally."

What she came bearing they already had. In their isolation, a hundred villages had taken up nonviolence. Each time she arrived at another one she was amazed that something so delicate and improbable could be born spontaneously in so many different places. She became more and more convinced of its rightness, not just because she saw it working but because in her nighttime outbreaks, when she cried for Kamal and Casey in a stranger's bed, the thought of a greater love was the only thing that calmed her down. She had expected to teach, but instead she was offered succor by the people who would be her students, and with every handful of berries or cold rice they shared she imbibed some of their optimism and faith.

"To be nameless is the ultimate act of resistance."

"And the police hate it," Fantom said. "We pick 'em up on the short wave, calling us Village X."

"What are your plans?"

"We want to make it impossible for them to keep up the wall."

"We have a lot of children in here, so we can't risk too much violence," Marie said. "We don't want to have shooting or tear gas."

"And you can't do a hunger strike."

"Right. What we do instead is block the gate, two bodies at a time."

"We get up when it's food convoys, or medical. Who's out there now?" he asked Marie.

"Lady G and Korrekt. When they come to do inspections, we lie across the entrance. They can pull us away, but it takes them a while to come to the decision, and in the meantime more people come up and lie down in the same place. They can drive over us, but that's messy for them."

"And for you."

Marie looked at Fantom. He said, "It kills the nigga under the truck."

"I'm so sorry," Lore said.

"We are what time has made us," said Marie. "And time will triumph in the end."

They bound her leg between wooden splints with scraps of flowered sheet. Fantom's little girl ran to the other end of the village for a single crutch. Lore howled when she put her foot on the ground. "Fucking mother of Christ!" She hopped around a little. Then she said, "I want to take a shift."

Fantom looked dubious. Marie said, "There's no reason for you to do that."

"Yes . . . there is," panted Lore. She squeezed the little girl's hand. "I'll be . . . the perfect problem."

She went out two days later. Two teenage boys helped lower her to the ground, and then Marie lay down with the crown of her head touching Lore's and her feet stretched in the opposite direction. The opening was exactly two people wide. Lore could feel the cement gatepost with the toes of her good foot. She looked up at the sky, which was a pale brilliant blue. She smelled cigarette smoke and heard the scrape of chairs on gravel; then she smelled beetroot coffee. The pleasant murmur of voices made her want to go to sleep. "Is it always a party?" she asked Marie.

"They're here to witness."

Turning her head, she saw that a dozen people had gathered about thirty feet away. She waved, and those who happened to be looking waved back. Lore folded her hands on her stomach. Her body from throat to groin felt very tender and exposed. She was cold. Her knee hurt. She thought of the person who had died here. How much pain would you feel as you were crushed? Would it end only at the moment you died, or at some point before that? She thought of the rumpled, time-softened paperback in her backpack. She had not sent it home with Kamal, believing in her pride that she would finish it with him when he was older, that they would sit together again discussing memory and art. But she was a human roadblock looking up into the sky. It was unlikely, she realized, that she would get back to Middle Hill. The path between here and Freesia Street seemed endless, and endlessly obstructed. Even if she succeeded in reaching the wall towns and then left them with her heart and body intact and doubled back west, there would be many, many more villages to visit, each with its particular imprint of sorrow and defiance; there would be many more Maries and Fantoms, like and unlike each other in every way. She didn't think she was necessarily the best person for this job, but she was on it. She would most likely never see Kamal again, nor Casey, nor Mattie with his life full of unexplained absences and secret ecstasies.

Their shift was almost over when the trucks came. Lore was in so much pain that her knee was all she could think about, even when the trucks ground to a halt and men stepped around her in the blinding sun. When they pulled her to her feet, she cried out. "She has a broken leg!" Marie shouted.

"I'm all right, I'm all right." She hopped with them to the rear of the convoy. They had to lift her up over the tailgate into the back of the truck, and then they dragged her into place against the metal wall and pulled her legs around front to sit her down. The floor of the trailer was corrugated, and every time her heel took another bump it was being hit on the knee with a pickaxe. She felt sweat start out on her forehead and roll down the sides of her eyes. A rushing sound filled her ears, and she rested her head against the wall and passed out.

Eras later, it seemed, she was drinking water from a paper cup. When the cup was empty she returned it to a light-skinned man in immaculate clothing—a buttoned shirt and clean jeans—who crunched it up and put it in his pocket. A police bent down and fastened her hands behind her with a plastic zip cord, which he then attached to one of the chains hanging from the truck wall. This raised her hands and sent stabbing pains through her upper arms and shoulders. The clean-dressed man sat on a folding chair. "Why don't you give us a minute?" he said to the police.

"I'll turn on this light for you."

"That would be very helpful."

The roll-down door made a thunderous sound. She and the clean-dressed man were alone with each other.

"What's your name?" he said.

She told him. "What's yours?"

"Eddie."

"You're working for the police?" she said. The clean man smiled. His teeth, she noticed, were in perfect shape. No, he said, not exactly. She ventured: "Can you get them to untie my hands? It really hurts."

"Sorry, I don't interfere with protocol."

He sounded white. Lore had been raised speaking standard English, but she knew she did not sound white. "I understand," she said. "But maybe you could ask them for some painkillers."

"Let's talk a little first."

Despite what she thought of as her empty-handedness— her tendency to arrive in new places with no news, no material aid and no advice—Lore was often approached by people who wanted to talk. They asked after loved ones lost in Enclosure, or related long stories of mistreatment by SAPIDAD. Sometimes they told her their personal problems. Last night she'd sat up with Fantom's daughter and her friends, answering their questions about schools and rules in other villages. "Sure, if you want," she said.

"You've been traveling for some time, correct?"

"About a year."

"And you're doing what, organizing rebellions?"

The discomfort in her upper body was taking over from her knee. She shifted position as much as she could. It built by the moment, filling her mind with the sense of tendons tearing and muscles separating, and becoming mentally as well as physically unbearable. She let out a small groan. "The sooner you answer, the sooner you get the pills," Eddie said.

Perplexity edged in under the pain. What kind of snitch was this? "We're building a coalition. Villages tend to have street associations or other organizational structures already in place." She tried shrugging her shoulders forward, then back. "So I just let them know that we can all coordinate with each other and work for change."

"What kind of change?"

"Nonviolent ... Eddie, I would really appreciate it if you could help me out."

He got off the chair and came and knelt right by her, peering into her face. His own was well-formed and handsome, with hazel eyes. She looked away, and Eddie took her chin and cheek in a cool grip and moved her face back to him. "I'm not here to help you out, Lore Henry," he said.

He was a different kind of person, she realized. The way he spoke, the way he moved—these were not the ways of anyone she had met before. Yet she knew he couldn't be a police. Sluggishly pushing through her preoccupation with pain, her brain worked out the alternatives. "Are you from outside?" she asked.

"I'm from a place where we don't hit prisoners," Eddie said. He resumed his seat. "Please don't make me call in the guard to do it for me."

Outside!

"What are the ultimate goals of your movement?"

"Liberation. Justice."

"Do you work with anyone from North Harbor?"

"From where?" Lore said. She rolled her head against the

wall. No relief. "Look, don't call in the—the guard. What-ever I know, I'll tell you. I don't have any secrets."

He seemed interested. "You'll tell me the details of the rebellion in the village?"

"It's what you see. They're using passive resistance to put the police in a position where they have to either open the wall or arrest the entire village."

"What makes you think they won't do that?"

"They might," she said. "I don't know."

"They might kill everyone there," Eddie said. He ran a hand over his leg, picking specks off the jeans. "I believe they would."

"Maybe, yeah."

"So are you guys suicidal or just nuts?"

"Not suicidal," Lore said. She smiled, thinking of coffee, the dedication with which every village produced its own blend of acorns, chicory, dandelion root or peas. "Must be nuts."

"I see." The clean man stood up. "Good luck to you."

"Why don't you join us, Eddie?"

"Join you?" he said, obviously amused.

"How many black people are left out there? It must get pretty lonely."

He raised his eyebrows. "You think I'm black?"

"You know what you are."

"Miss Henry, I suggest you ask yourself which one of us is chained up in the back of a truck," he said. "Then think about who's black."

He knocked, and the door rolled up. Before it rolled down again, he turned off the light.

6

She was a different person when the trial ended. Weaker, more frightened, a hundred times more abased, yet simultaneously closer, as if separated only by a membrane, to that pinpoint of steel which was most palpable to her when she was most without hope. It was merely a point; it had no dimensions, nothing she could clutch to herself, it did not speak of God. But it existed, and that made two of them.

Her crimes were traveling on an expired pass and violating an ESC, or emergency safety cordon. During the trial, she grew in knowledge. She learned that the ID readers carried by police were also capable of making telephone calls, playing audio recordings and transmitting written messages. She learned that white people ate constantly, crinkling brightly colored wrappers or plucking nuts from secret pockets, and that they drank coffee all day out of plastic mugs. This taught her that occupiers are a nervous race, craving stability, whose sense of themselves must be continually fortified. She learned too that everything she had seen outside these walls was the intentional result of a vast legal structure—a machinery of suffering which it took a whole nation to operate and which she knew, but could not believe, was constructed entirely to generate profit.

They shaved her head, took her clothes, gave her baggy gray underwear and olive scrubs and a pair of rubber shoes without socks. They weighed and measured her and stuck an adhesive bar code on the back of her hand and scanned it. They took her from the court building through an underground passage—she had not smelled fresh air in weeks—into a chamber made of cement, lit with fluorescents, in which she was again weighed and measured, again interrogated (name, age, crime, qualification status) and scanned. She was in plastic handcuffs; she had not been out of them, except to pee, since Eddie had her locked up in the truck. Her wrists were skinned, on fire. They put her in a cell with one fluorescent bulb overhead and a metal door with a small wired window just above her eye level. They cut off the handcuffs streaked with her brown blood. She had a mattress on an iron frame, a toilet and a flat metal shelf above it. The ceiling was cement, the walls were cement, the floor was cement and the whole thing was painted dark gray. They shut the door. She was sentenced to five months solitary. She could not breathe.

The routine was this: oatmeal and water at six. Exercise at ten. Bread, beef broth and apple juice at one. Canned peas or corn, one slice of meat, water at six. Lights out at ten. On Sunday, a piece of candy. On Tuesday, a wash.

She went mad. It was not too bad for a while. She knew how to loosen the tiny frantic fingers of her mind from their clutch on her self. She sat on the floor in the middle of the cell and breathed evenly and felt the blood tingling in her fingers and toes. She looked closely at every bit of the walls within her height, tracing minute flaws and pockmarks in the cement, and she listened to the faint sounds carried from elsewhere in the prison: a shouted syllable, a throb of footsteps, the echo of a door closing. She did sit-ups, crunching her shoulder blades against the floor. She walked the cell and counted her steps. She counted out the seconds taken for exercise: fifteen to twenty-three for the guard to enter her cell and shackle her, between one hundred and ten and one hundred and seventeen to walk down the corridor and take a right turn to the exercise cubicle, eleven to twelve to enter the cubicle, twenty-four seconds (twenty-eight steps) to make a circuit of the cubicle, forty-one to forty-two circuits. She counted the peas: an average of ninety-three. Corn, an average of eighty. It was difficult to decide which fraction to assign to each smushed or partial pea. They rolled around and she accidentally crushed them with her fingers and had to start again. Sometimes there were soft translucent husks and she didn't know whether to count them as peas or not. She got angry, horribly angry, when there were too many of these; it haunted her that SAPIDAD would not even give her whole peas, she could barely sleep at night. And sleep was her only fraction of happiness. So she had to stop counting, and that was when she began to lose control.

She had panic attacks so terrible they were like seizures, during which she tried to scream for help but could not. She slept for long dead periods, sleep that was scant and sour but held her like a straitjacket. When she got up she could not remember what she had been doing to keep herself together, and her mind wobbled and flitted brokenly from one half-formed thought to another. Sometimes there was movement out of the corner of her eye. At last she saw it, a large beetle running up the cell wall. She got close and examined its white-tipped antennae and its ridged purply-green carapace. When she tried to touch it, it seemed to move to another section of the wall. She watched for a long time. The next day she asked the guard if there were any beetles in the prison. He didn't seem to hear her. She began to hear them scratching inside the walls. She felt them crawling on her in bed, thousands of hinged legs running over her body. Her screaming and banging finally brought two guards who inspected the cell and, furious to have their sleep disturbed, hooded her and shackled her to the toilet.

She knew her name, her age, knew her parents were dead. But she didn't really know who she was. Lore was a word for something empty. It even sounded empty, with a hole in the middle. Her past was a picture on a wall.

Once she dreamed about Cay and woke up electrified. He had been in her cell, telling her to hold on. She realized she could reconstruct him exactly, from his small jutting beard to his stocky toes, from his rumbly chuckle to the feel of his hand on her ass. She could make herself come, silently and almost without movement on the prison mattress, just by imagining him touching her wretched body.

She came and came as the guard-eye came and went. He would joke about it, asking her if he was nothing but a sex toy.

I don't want to keep you here, she said. She heard her own voice in her head, and she heard his. Sometimes she moved her lips just a little, not enough for the guard to see. I'm here to help you, Cay said. Do with me what you will.

I don't want to ... you know. She meant, desecrate the living person.

What choice do you have? said Cay. You might come out of this alive.

He stayed in the cell while she exercised. Each time she came back she described the changes in the outside world. The mop in the corridor is gone. Nazareth was in a bad mood. He only let me do thirty-nine circuits.

I'll rip his head off, Cay said.

Remember, we all about the nonviolence here.

What good did it do you? No, she said, you wouldn't be like that, you supported my dad. On the outside, said Cay. Not here in Central Hell. Your mama was right, he needed a pair of balls.

And your mama, she had more than either of them. Auntie Iris.

She dead too. It Hell East out by the wall now. Let's not talk about that, she said. Let's talk about you. You ain't want to hear it, he said. Let's have it, asshole. Well, I got married. I'll rip *her* head off. Hey, he said, nonviolence.

Who is it, Tanya?

Nah Michelle.

I don't like that.

You asked, he said.

With his help she became steady again, and the formlessness of her prison experience drew together and coalesced into a solid shape, starting with the trial and continuing with a chain of black nights and fluorescent days. Together they calculated that she had been in solitary for about three weeks. Oh Mary, she said, mother of God, help me.

We get through it. They worked on a mental model of SAPIDAD. She needed something, he said, a project.

Skeptical at first, she found to her surprise that she knew more about the regime's operations than she thought she did. She knew the territory—SAPID—comprised thirteen buckets, widely scattered, each containing about ten clusters of a dozen to fifteen factories; three groupings of relatively populous towns, one at the wall, one in the hills, and one on the southern coastline; hundreds of villages; and long expanses of lonely country, from the northern stretch where gangs ruled to the farmland in the interior. Highways built by SAPIDAD connected the buckets to each other and to the import processing zones to the north and west of SAPID.

I bet you know the personnel too.

Well, there are supervisors. And lieutenants, like the one who killed Russ and Deshawn. There are probably captains and majors over the lieutenants. And above them …

Colonels and generals.

But who do the generals report to?

You tell me.

What is outside the wall?

You tell me.

That man, Eddie.

I make an exception for him, Cay said. Kick his mulatto face in when I sees him next.

He wasn't SAPIDAD. You could tell by the way he talked.

What's out there?

A society of Eddies.

She became less and less interested in reality. Being with Cay was the rational choice. When his image faltered, the pressure of real life was excruciating: it hurt to exist. The only way to hold back the sluicing accumulation of despair was to return immediately to her pretend world. She understood that she could go on this way for months—the image might not even decay—but she would not belong in the world when it was over. She gave herself two more days. Then five, then ten. She could not let him go. She let him go, and almost died of it.

7

Muggy in driving rain, awash with meaningless sounds, the world was not nearly as kind as solitary had been at last. She missed her walls, her floor, even the guard whose whispers had helped sustain her, who had taken her home for a night and given her money and pointed the way to the wall towns. She missed the peace she had learned to wear like nakedness, the knowledge that she was in the necessary place doing the necessary thing. Solitary was a permanent disfiguration, like having a leg cut off. She was not sure what shape of person she was now.

This place had been shelled. It would have been busy once, but as she walked down the center of a wide avenue lined by frontless buildings and carcasses of cars, with the rain rattling like sheet metal around her, she saw only lame dogs and furtive humans pushing shopping carts. Twenty years of decay had crumbled walls like charcoal and grown a skirt of pulpy refuse around every remaining structure. The rain acted like a drill, releasing sewage that overflowed the gutters and seeped into her shoes. In the roadblocks formed from rubble, in gun barrels extruding from windows, in the atmosphere of ceaseless warfare she read the presence of the Brothers.

She turned off the avenue to find a place to sleep. Nothing seemed real—not the pools of fetid liquor that rose above her ankles nor the fallen fences that scored her flesh as she climbed over them. She huddled beneath a leaning wall and dreamed of prison. When she woke, it seemed exactly the same hour of lightless day. Although she felt neither hunger nor thirst, she reached for her pack, took out a piece of the jerky she had bought two towns ago, ate it, unscrewed the cap from her bottle of water and drank some. She unfolded a knife and cut a line across her forearm. Blood welled in the cut. She wrapped her arm in a shirt and picked up the pack.

The rain had stopped. She walked east through an abandoned scrapyard still ruled by taxonomy: axle with rusted axle, I-beam with I-beam in a land where no one came looking for parts. A small animal was trapped in a tangle of rebar torn from its mortar roots. Could she eat it? She had to put down her pack to crawl in. "Well, I'll be fucked," she said, shocked by the sound of her own voice.

She washed it as best she could with bottled water and carried it back to the avenue. The child nodded its burning head against her cheek. It spoke words she did not catch, in a low, guttural voice, and writhed. "Keep still, now," Lore said. It was the most noxious bundle she had ever carried. She put it down at the foot of a barricade.

"Dysentery," said the Brother who came out.

"Where's the hospital?"

"Move along now."

"Hospital? You know? Where they treats children on the verge of death?"

"Go on down to the city center."

"Ain't no center there," she said. "You know that, right? You know it ain't nothing there but debris and some citizens scared out they mind."

"Look, I've asked you twice to move. This is a dangerous area for you to be in."

"How long the Brothers been holding this town? Long enough to get some sanitation in here? Long enough to get some kind of medical clinic together, you think?"

He raised the gun and pointed it at her. "Crazy lady, you need to move along."

"Y'all won't be satisfied until this whole territory is a pile of shit," Lore said. She picked up the child and went.

In the gigantic shell of a movie theater, a fixer sold her twelve dusty white pills in a baggie. She made a bed for the child in the balcony, fed her more water and an antibiotic, and watched her. She was a small person about Kamal's age with a shrunken, lined face, deeply circled under the eyes, which were yellow when they opened and stared at Lore. Her clothes—a checked shirt and red-stitched jeans—had once been well cared for, and her awful hair betrayed a foundation of cornrows. In her pockets were a kitchen knife and a lump of flaked mud that turned out to be crackers. She slept arduously, moaning and crying out by turns, breath squeaking in her throat, and her body, however often Lore cleaned it, stank of adult sweat.

"In the bowl, hon. That's it." She carried it down a flight of stairs blasted open to the wind and hazy sun. Buried the muck in a dirt lot half a block away. Bargained with a toothless woman for a twist of instant soup. The fixer had a can of Sterno and matches, and between them, within an hour, they managed to heat a cup of black-market water almost to warmth.

The fixer was seventeen and, after two days, hopelessly in love with Lore. He was much too soft-hearted to have a future in business. She let him hold her in the seats next to the child's. His erection was proof of the world outside herself, a sprouting of the same dumb animal nature that had her taking care of the child and would carry her away from here. His mama was dead, his sisters dead or with the Brothermen. His cousins, friends all gone, his number-one homes killed right up against that wall. Until she asked him to stop talking because she was not listening, she was just a bony animal hearing sounds and registering sensations like the push of his dick or the wetness of his spasmodic tears. When the police came she shouldered her bundle and left him.

Reka, R-E-K-A. Grosvenor: G-R-O, silent S, V-E-N-O-R.
"Was your grandma qualified, sweetheart?"
"What?"
"Did she have an ID card?"
"The polices took her."
"I know, darling." So the child was undocumented, and the grandmother must have been too. Lore had met that

grandmother. Not A-L-O-U-E-T-T-E but a dozen like her, broad-shouldered women raising the children of Enclosure while practicing, each in her own way, a tenacious resistance to the regime that had destroyed the first generation and condemned the second to a life behind walls. She knew Reka would never see her grandmother again.

They lived for a week inside the stripped husk of a school bus about a mile out of town. She made a bed for Reka in the aisle, between the twisted frameworks of the missing seats. In the morning they heard birds, in the evening crickets. In the afternoons gunfire. Reka was a scrupulous child, hampered by thought. Her life with Alouette had been well-regulated and she clearly hoped for, but did not presume to expect, the same from Lore. She waited patiently to recover, drinking the soup Lore brought, agreeing that her tummy was not so bad today, convulsing silently in her effort to swallow the last antibiotic and then saying, "That tasted pretty good." Her eyes left Lore for longer than a minute only when she was asleep, and she knew it. The heavy, drape-like quality of her devotion was horrible to both of them, for different reasons.

They were easiest with each other over the Twain. "It was in Warwick Castle," Lore read, "that I came across the curious stranger whom I am going to talk about." Reka did not interrupt as Kamal had. She listened in stillness to what must have been nearly incomprehensible, her survivor's mind working steadily, sturdily towards meaning. She would be all right on her own. She just needed some help, and everything that did not involve Lore's heart was available on the black market.

"'You know about transmigration of souls; do you know about transposition of epochs—and bodies?'"

She was the burden that Lore was not willing to bear.

8

By the time she was arrested again, she knew what would happen. She had spoken to enough ex-cons to get their stories by heart: solitary confinements longer than her own; interrogations without limit; torture administered like medicine by men who consulted guidelines on little screens. SAPIDAD's prisons were decontamination chambers, purpose-built to eradicate mites infecting the body capital. Lore was one of many mites. She brought news of the Coalition to the villages, and in return villagers taught her the technicalities of survival—how to repair a generator, construct a sewage system, treat cholera, make soap. They taught her how they governed themselves, whom they entrusted with the right to make decisions and how they held those trusted leaders to account. She wrote on any paper she could find, crossing old newsprint with accounts of her travels and sending them to the seat of the Coalition in the south. To Ira she wrote, "We are too top-down on Freesia St. I see villages out here where even children have a vote. How can we engage the rest of our neighbors and empower them?" Communication between councils being slow, even as couriers and radio operators were added daily, it was weeks before she received his reply, which did not mention empowerment but reported that Cay and Tanya had twins. "Come back to your family," he wrote in a stranger's hand, "and let Deedee go on the road, she needs the seasoning."

She spent a second winter in the buckets, canvassing the slums. She was frequently accused of being a snitch and even more frequently told she didn't know nothing about nothing. She got to know many Miss Mindys, not all of whom promoted prostitution, although some did. They were the best-informed women in their communities: they knew who hated life in the bucket and who accepted it, who yearned for change and who preferred sleep, alcohol or gem. With their help Lore found shelter and—usually through their contacts in the Brotherhood—fake IDs. She joined factory lines, keeping the same hours and obeying the same rules as the workers she sought to organize. She waited with these workers in company stores and signed away her paycheck, as they did, for onions and bread. She listened and listened and listened, and only then did her co-workers really talk. Many of them had already heard about the villages where there were no factories, where you could build your own house, grow your own food, and help educate your and your neighbors' children. Yes, she said, those places were not far away, and she could tell them how to get there. She told them about the Coalition, and about the ultimate goal of mass economic refusal which would bring down the factories. At this point, if she was called an ignorant motherfucker again, it was kindly. And if she and Miss Janine or Miss Angie arranged a meeting, people showed up. And if the police came too, someone was usually willing to boost her out the back window.

Although she knew what SAPIDAD could do to her, she was not at present afraid. She gave herself fully to the miracle of people, their vast number and endless variation—their different faces and the way they stood and their separate heartaches and the awesome power of their united will. She knew she would never have children, because the children who already existed in the world were so splendid they filled her to bursting. (Just in case, though, and also because it was mostly women who surrounded her, she mostly slept with women.) Two years after solitary, she found the natural world so beautiful that everything from a frozen puddle to green weeds rising through shattered tarmac could stop her stride. She loved to hear raindrops drum a tin roof beneath which she and some comrade sat talking, filling each other with hope.

Crocuses appeared on the roadside, purple and pebble-white. Ira wrote, "Their names are Victoria and Vincent, and they want to meet their godmother."

"Vincent?" she said to Cay when she saw him next. "Victoria?"

"Tanya picked them."

She opened her legs and took his cock in a second time, fitting around it so perfectly she felt him convulse with rapture and regret. The outflux shook him like a puppy, and he wept into her open eyes.

"How old am I?"

"Twenty-one," said her father's oldest friend. He handed her a joint.

Freesia Street was built on a hill, and they stood on top of it, looking east toward the border. The wall bisected their vision from side to side, a black bulk zipping up the horizon, tightly sealed except for one pucker of outline that suggested buildings. "What is that?" she asked him.

"A city."

"On this side?"

"Have you ever heard of a city with skyscrapers on this side?"

"Is it North Harbor?"

Ira said, "This all was. From where we're standing right down to the bay."

She lit up with her matches and flint. "Why aren't we organizing there?"

"Where?"

"In North Harbor."

"You mean aside from the military installation between us and them?"

"A thought experiment," Lore said.

"It's been twenty years," Ira said. "Nobody knows what North Harbor is like now."

"I do," she said. "It's a prosperous white city on the edge of SAPID. The quantity of goods coming over must be astronomical. The people are politically unengaged, amoral, self-absorbed, racist, conformist, and materialistic."

"You sound like you want to shoot them, not organize them."

"Most of them have grown up thinking we're terrorists, right? They're petrified. They have to have their material things to distract them, or they wouldn't be able to live with the fear. They can't afford to be moral, because they'd have to renounce their entire lifestyle. They're racist and materialistic because that's what the culture has taught them to be."

Ira held out his hand for the joint. "You may be right."

"I think we should go over there," Lore said.

"Why?"

"It's right there, Ira. They could help us."

"You want white people to fund this revolution?"

"Who said anything about funding? They have other resources. A court system."

"Your father always told us not to rely on outsiders."

"A little money wouldn't be the end of the world," Lore said.

She remembered when children raced each other down this slope, screaming with joy. Now the street was deserted. The electricity had been cut while she was away and never restored. Helicopters churned and tore the air for hours at a time, leading to a state of communal unease in which no conversation was begun with the expectation that it would be finished. Sleep was broken by distant gunfire, spurts of sound that bedeviled the night. People were stressed. The stewards of the street association tried to sort out a response by candlelight. They were Lore, Ira, Deedee, Levander and Cay, until Cay's wife forbade him to see Lore and Levander disappeared.

For the police were here now. They set up barricades not only on the street itself but on the paths around it, among the ruins of old townhouses and the overgrown storefronts, where they congregated in their bulky nylon jackets, muttering into readers. The sight of them perspiring in the late-summer sun might have been funny had they not been so many, and so huge. Each pair of black-clad shoulders was twice as big around as Lore. They drove jeeps down the street which had not seen a car in two decades, jerking and bouncing over potholes and swerving right at anyone unlucky enough to be outside. They came at midnight, looking for IDs. If IDs were not produced they smashed windows, ripped up gardens and burned books and papers. They did this all without rage, meticulously. "Better get to a bucket," they said on leaving, or, "Plenty of jobs in the factories." Occasionally they took someone with them, and that was what had happened to Levander.

"What's the point?" said Deedee, her face streaked with tears. "We could let them slaughter all of us, and no one would ever know."

"We have no other choice."

"Than to be slaughtered?" Nobody had been shot so far, but nobody believed it wasn't coming. "For whose benefit, Ira? Who would even see?" The people around her nodded their heads. "Nonviolence is a means of persuasion," one man said. "And ain't no motherfuckers left to persuade."

"Nonviolence is a commitment," Ira roared. "Not a means to an end!"

"Listen," Lore said. Because the kitchen was so crowded, she got up on a rickety chair. "There are always people left to persuade. Police are people. They can feel shame and sorrow. And they know right from wrong."

"You go up to that police that took Levander and you ask him do he feel shameful, and he shoot you in the head!"

"They are animals," a woman said. "Cockroaches," said another.

"I'm not saying it will stop them. But they're human—we have to hold onto that. Deedee, you're wrong that nobody would know. People in the south and the west and the north will hear what we did, and they'll do the same when it's their turn. If we're peaceful, everything we do here, under the gun, helps our movement all across the territory. But if we react with violence, we fragment it. People lose faith, they join the Brothers and abandon their councils, or they smuggle in weapons and try to kill police, and they fail, and the movement degenerates into one-sided skirmishes that wipe us out while SAPIDAD stays in control. We're trying to change the way the world works," she said, "and you don't do that with guns."

There was something more. She did not yet know how to communicate this, but it seemed to her that each of them was also responsible for her own soul, and because she did not believe in heaven it also seemed to her that one's soul resided in those last instants of awareness, and she did not want them swollen with hate. Indeed, she could not have borne the prospect of her own death if she thought it would come on a wave of bitterness.

Not that she was unafraid to die. The fear took hold at odd moments, paralyzing her with a horror so immense it blacked out everything else and left her sick and weak. Nothing, she felt, could be worse than that fear, not even death itself.

She was arrested on a September morning and taken in an armored vehicle north along the wall for what she judged to be fifty or sixty miles. The men in the car appeared to know her; they addressed her, brusquely, as Henry. At the end of the ride she was lifted down (her hands and feet were shackled) onto a glaringly hot tarmac covered with folding tables and tents. Shuffling prisoners were being processed slowly through the maze of tables and shunted towards a barbed-wire gate beyond which stood rows of Quonset huts and, rising above them, a large, gleaming building of pure white.

"Name?"

"Lore Henry."

"ID number?"

"I do not accept your system of numbering human beings."

"Zatz? I have an eleven-C here."

"Name?"

"Lore Henry."

"ID six oh six three oh?"

"I do not accept—"

"I need an admit for eleven-C, tent eight. Get your butt over here."

"Name?"

"You know, I'm in your computer. I've been in prison before."

"Six oh six three oh. Fast-tracked for processing at the Vet."

"Don't you have one of those little bar code thingies? So I don't have to keep answering your questions over and over?"

"You think it's funny now, Henry?" said the police seated behind the table. "You won't think so for very long."

"You may be right," she said.

The hut was divided into cells with a sort of chicken wire, thin but rigid, which reached almost to the domed ceiling. Each cell was large enough for one person to lie down in and contained a security camera and a metal bucket. There were thirty of them—three rows of ten, with two narrow aisles. The hut was dark and very hot. When a door opened at either end, the sunlight could blind whomever it struck, while the rest of them remained in darkness.

She had biblical neighbors: Rebecca on one side, Esther on the other. Kendra beyond Esther, Robyn beyond Bec. Yolanda, Seely, Judy, Khadijah, and a girl who called herself Soldier in the middle, and others beyond those. They were the Pussy Cabin, and Pussy Cabin took care of its own. They wondered how their jailers had come to make such a damaging mistake. Perhaps SAPIDAD believed that black men, if imprisoned next to black women, would tear down partitions to rape them and thus deprive policemen of their lawful work.

Not every day, but on many days, Lore was taken to the Vet. It was well-named, being as organized and sanitary as an animal hospital, except that the men there would not have done to an animal what they did to her. They were good men. They had rules to follow, as they often told her—statues, regulations, legal decisions. The latticework of oversight was so all-pervasive, it was a wonder they got anything done. But they stuck with it. They were all trained, they told her, in survival, evasion, resistance, and escape; what she was experiencing, each of them had experienced. And she, being their victim, was spared the extensive instruction they had been obliged to endure, the seminars in legality, accountability, variability, quantifiability, and restraint. "I have a fucking Ph.D. in this here," one of them informed her amiably, "so you don't got nothing to worry about."

They hung her; stretched her; leaned her on her fingertips. That was the real subject of their study: how to force her body closer and closer to what it could not do, so that the possible strained to touch the impossible and the space between them was filled with the natural excretion of that pressure, which was pain. Then, also, they hurt her directly. She soiled herself. She vomited on them, and they hurt her again.

They attached alligator clips to the tender flaps of her body. Her organs turned inside out. Her teeth ground to powder inside her shattering head. On that chair she was no one, not even their slave.

IV

THE PIANO FACTORY

Lemon cake

When she looked out the window, she couldn't believe her eyes. There was her face, or what she had come to accept was her face, on a low-rising billboard in the middle of the parking lot, and stamped across it were the livid words:

MY SOUL IS NOT FOR SALE
MY JEANS ARE NO NAME
LOLLYWORLD ON 5TH STREET

That was it? That was what she'd been stolen from her home for, that was why they kept her prisoner and painted her skin and shot her with cameras, and why she was here in this horrible apartment with the lady who wouldn't stop crying? Jeans?

She went into the living room, where Aimee was still asleep, and took her tap-tap. Then she went into the kitchen and opened all the cabinets, stuck her fingers in the sugar bowl and licked them, went through the contents of the refrigerator and turned on the coffee machine.

"North Harbor University Reimbursements Department."

"Hello, may I please speak with Sterling?" Her grandmother had once owned a telephone and Reka remembered her manners, unlike some.

"Hold on," said the voice. In a minute it came back and said, disapprovingly, "Sterling no longer works here."

"Oh," Reka said, and instantly underwent the kind of collapse of confidence—like a vacuuming-out of her will—that occurred several times a day: "Do, do ..."

"I don't have any more information," said the voice, and then added, not unkindly, "Try Directory."

She tried Directory. She was getting better at the God-damn things, but they were so slippery and her fingers were unlearned. For a while she couldn't remember Sterling's last name. NOTHING MATCHED YOUR SEARCH. She had to wake Aimee up and ask her.

"Oh, angel, she doesn't have a tap-tap." She reached her arms out longingly, which Reka couldn't stand. It made her feel like a doll or something. "Why don't you wait and I'll go over to her house after work."

"Work started an hour ago," she said, and Aimee said, "Oh God, oh God," and rolled off the couch. Then at least Reka was alone, but she had no tap-tap. She poured coffee into one of Aimee's bright yellow mugs, added spoonfuls of sugar and a gob of the special cream Aimee had gotten her (it tasted like maple syrup), took two pieces of lemon sparkly cake and went across the hall.

He had warned her never to leave the apartment, Jamie who wasn't here now. He said she should not even look out the window. "Legally, your situation is extremely precarious. In a sense you don't even have a legal situation, because you have no rights. I realize it may be hard for you to hear this, but I want you to understand." The reason he wasn't here was that he and Aimee could not stop fighting. "That's why we can't sue Coyson for unlawful restraint or theft of wages. What we can do is sue them for unfair business practices, and we're talking to a potential plaintiff today. Then as soon as we file, we petition that the government be enjoined from detaining you due to its relationship with Sirocco, which as Coyson's corporate parent is a party to the case. Do you understand what I'm saying?"

"How can you petition the government to enjoin itself?" Aimee said.

"Years of practice," Jamie said. "Reka, do you understand?"

She understood all right. Somebody ought to tell these people slavery was over. Though she wasn't sure it really was—she would like to ask Lore about that.

She gave Zaiden a piece of cake when he answered the door. Zaiden was fifteen, three years older than she was. You could tell he was really a girl, but he didn't like for you to mention that. He shaved every morning, even though there was nothing to shave, and he wore a thick nylon undershirt to keep his boobs down. He had cowboy boots like Edmark's but she didn't mind. Zaiden had been very surprised the first time he saw her. Then he wanted to bring a court case, just like Jamie, but she explained that wouldn't be necessary. She was going back any day now.

They munched cake and looked things up on Zaiden's tap-tap. There wasn't much about Sirocco, which Zaiden said was because Sirocco was everything; if you were on the moon you didn't need a definition of the moon, did you? Reka wasn't sure. She looked up the name everybody used for her home and found out it meant Special Assistance Perimeter Interim District. *SAPID No. 1 was formed in 2003 to aid recovery from the <u>terrorist attacks</u> and subsequent <u>counter-strikes</u> that devastated western New England.* "Everybody knows that's bullshit," Zaiden said.

"They do?"

"Yeah, I mean, we're middle-class but we're not stupid."

"Then why don't people do something about it?"

He pushed back a lock of pale hair with his thin girl's hand. Sometimes the hand trembled, as his voice trembled when he spoke to her, and she understood he felt his place in the world to be easily shattered. "Uh," he said, "lazy?"

They looked up a map of SAPID and zoomed in towards the railroad tracks, and she grew frustrated when the picture grayed out. "I want to see my house."

"I thought you were homeless," Zaiden said.

"I have a house," Reka said. She pinched her fingers on the screen and smalled the tracks. The place names and boundaries came into view again, and she studied the wall that curved between her current location and her home. "Someone fucked with it. I'm going to fuck them."

"Up?"

"What?"

"Fuck them up? Or fuck them?" Zaiden said. "It's two different things."

She said nothing. He reached over and tapped up a

picture of a naked white girl. "I think about fucking a lot," he said. "A lot."

They looked at the picture in silence. Reka felt strange. She wondered if black girls didn't get hair in that place. "I call her Lisa," said Zaiden after a while. "And I talk to her. I know that's pathetic."

"It's okay."

He looked at her, and moved the hair from his face again.

"I used to have girls too," Reka said.

She liked him, but he was just a kid. She needed to talk to Sterling.

Day 22

She remembered the first time she became aware of popshow. She was about three years old, eating her favorite cookie, Chip-a-roos, and her mother put on the Chip-a-roo show. Back then there were no hypes as such: cookies did not dance and sing on the actual surface of the package, but each bag came with a little disc or "show," which you could pop into your TV to see a cookie dancing and singing "Chip-a-roos are good for youse." She remembered watching, horrified, and letting the half-masticated cookie drool out of her mouth, and when she saw for sure that it was the same as the confection on the screen she began to vomit. It felt like she'd been tricked into eating some soft, malignant creature. After that she would not touch any kind of food that came in a package. They were dirty, she said when she was taken to the doctor—the cookies, the macaroni, the carrots, the ham. She ate so little she had to be hospitalized, and there in her sunny room were more crawling, creeping creatures, unnatural smiles on their faces and their encouraging words piped in by speaker: *Sneaky Sandwich says get well soon! Wash your hands with Li'l Squirt Soap. Do you like Dorma-dolls? Tell Mom to run downstairs and get you some!* She grew worse. She was put in isolation, and they were in isolation too. *L'il Squirt will keep you clean!*

She lost two years of her childhood that way. She considered her family essentially brainless, and the day she graduated from college she broke off all contact with them.

It never got better, but she got better at dealing with it. She majored in math, because as much as popshow invaded the texts and screens she used for studying, it could not touch mathematical truth. When she was twenty-one, she met Aimee. Aimee was starting a campus group to resist trends in American society—according to her, government corruption, voter disenfranchisement, and the personhood movement for corporations—and Sterling was sure it would attract people like herself. Instead, she walked into a room full of hippies in Blue Revelation T-shirts. The only thing that ever brought her peace was the slow and steady work of sabotage, and Cleveland had put an end to that. Now every piece of popshow in the city was drilling little holes in her brain. LUXURY HAS A NEW NAME. ESCAPE THE ORDINARY. PAMPER YOUR-SELF. STAND OUT IN A CROWD. THE HOME YOU'VE ALWAYS WANTED. A CAR YOU CAN BELIEVE IN. DREAM YOURSELF INTO OUR JEANS. She was getting bored into non-existence.

"The question on the table is how we respond to what happened on Monday."

A young man put up his hand. "Can I just say, I think the police behaved very professionally."

"Excuse me?" Aimee said.

"I mean, she was here illegally. They basically had to arrest her."

"And you think they did that professionally?"

"I thought they were very respectful."

"Does anyone else have something useful to say?"

"I don't think we can discount Brendan's point," said a sweaty-faced man. "Whatever is done, has to be done within the law."

"Is it within the law to segregate America into black and white?" Aimee said. "Into rich and poor? Into people who are exploited and terrorized and—and us?"

"I think it's reductive to focus on race," someone said. "The fact is, this was done within the law, and it was done to help people. There wasn't a single criterion."

"So you think it's a coincidence that ninety-eight per-cent of the people of color in North Harbor were moved into SAPID?"

"It was based on assessed disadvantage. My cousin was

one of the people who worked on the algorithm. It took into account all sorts of things, like living conditions, access to health care, economic stability. I mean it even measured how impacted you were by the bombings, on a scale of one to fifty."

"And I ask you again, it's just a coincidence that the bombs mostly hit areas that were already disadvantaged?"

"You're not a conspiracy theorist, are you, Aimee?" a woman said. Aimee's face started to turn pink. The young man said, "I mean, I hear your passion, but there are already programs in place for people like Lore. She had legal avenues."

"And there are plenty of black people in North Harbor. It's not like they were eradicated," the sweaty man said. Someone else said, "And Latins."

"We don't even have proof of anything she said in that speech," the woman added. "I'm sorry, but we don't."

Aimee spoke slowly and clearly. "What we saw two days ago," she said, "was a person being dragged away, in *our* neighborhood, in *our* city, for telling us the truth about what's happening over the wall. Our lives can never be the same."

"I don't see how they can be any different, frankly," said the woman. Like most of them she was between forty and sixty, pleasantly dressed in well-kept, slightly unfashionable clothes. "We can't, like, go on a hunger strike to get her out of jail."

"Why not?" Aimee said.

"Well, *you* can," said the woman and laughed. "But I have a dinner party on Sunday."

"Isn't there anyone here who feels a sense of urgency?" One or two of them picked at their cheese and Gingham-FreshFarms grapes. Aimee looked around. "Lore has devoted her entire life to making change in the world," she said. "At a cost we can't even begin to comprehend. What have you done, Melody? What have any of us ever really done?"

The young man put up his hand again, and with an air of magnanimity said, "I suggest we reach out to our contacts at City Hall."

Sterling went outside. She was going to have to take up smoking if this went on—if her life continued to be reduced to a puny round of impotence and waiting. Maybe she could stick enough branded cigarettes into her mouth to die of logo poisoning. Cleveland was in the yard of this suburban house, leaning against a tree.

"How is the leftist coalition tonight?" he said.

"They couldn't coalesce around a piece of flypaper," Sterling said. "What do you want?"

"I have a message for you."

"Find any evidence?"

"Give me your hand."

"Go to hell."

"Don't be so antagonistic, Sterling. We need to avoid the cameras."

He held out his hand, slightly curled in the dark. She put hers in it and felt the folded edge of a piece of paper. "Don't read it here," he said. "Take it home, somewhere safe."

"You're so full of shit."

"I want you to consider something." He gripped her hand, and she knew, without any consideration at all, how satisfying it was for him to have her in the palm of his. "The risk I took getting that to you. I smuggled it out of a very secure facility. I could lose my job."

"I suppose you stored it up your ass?" She removed her hand. "Anything for the people."

"Don't you want to know how she is?" Cleveland said. "Health and spirits, that sort of thing?"

Sterling shrugged. "She's nothing to me."

"I see." He took out his tap-tap and, using it as both light and mirror, made a fine adjustment to his tie. "I told you about our reach," he said. "Anybody who so much as passed her in the street while she was here is going to be put under a very strong microscope."

"Except for me."

"I'll protect you while I can."

"That is truly touching," Sterling said.

It didn't bother her that Lore was in trouble. Lore had done what she came to do in full knowledge of the consequences. It would have taken a miracle for her to get away after that speech, and the miracle hadn't happened. What bothered Sterling was that even though Lore was gone she hadn't left. She still heard that practiced, insinuating voice, still saw the dark and crooked figure poised to step forward from a corner of the room. She still felt Lore's warm pressure on her flank in bed. Why did this vagabond presence persist? They had known each other just under a week. Why was that enough to uncouple Sterling's eye from reality?

She opened the message on the train. Care had been taken to make the handwriting clear and precise, but the stems of the letters were minutely jagged, and the paper was pocked with tiny irregularities from a rough surface. She read it once, then a second time. "Oh, my god," she said softly, "you unbelievable whore."

Letter of recommendation
Give to Ira Biggs on Freesia Street.

Dear Ira,

This is Sterling Teacher. She is a saboteur who has attacked many businesses in North Harbor, including Koisin Stone. I understand she can get into any building, no matter how secure. She has a photographic memory. She is also skilled in a number of useful techniques such as surveillance, eavesdropping, computer hacking, electronics and lying.

All my love goes to you and Alice and Cay and Tanya and their children.

I am not sure she will ever be any good at non-violence.

Love.

Red

A woman's touch on her cheek, soft and nectar-smelling: Lady Hazel, rousing her for the morning toilette. Lady, where have you been? I was detained, Your Majesty, most grievously detained. But I swear on my life I will not leave you again.

"Darling, wake up," a white person whispered. She saw Aimee leaning over her. "Angel, I'm sorry," she whispered. "You have to hide."

She jerked away and sprang to the far end of the bed, the one enclosed in the closet. From there she jumped, grabbing the edge of the highest shelf, and pulled herself up. She leaned out and furiously motioned Aimee to pull the bed away. Crouched in the low space, she shuffled back and back until she reached the wall, squirmed behind a suitcase, pulled her arms tight around herself and rolled on her side. Shocks of heat and cold went through her body, and her heart was pumping so fast she could feel her blood crashing like waves.

They were at the front door. She tucked her head down and lay like she was dead. Forcing the breath which struggled against her, willing it silently in and out of her mouth.

"My lawyer is on the way."

"This is a matter of national security, ma'am. A lawyer is not going to do you any good."

"I can't let you in until I see my lawyer."

"If you'll please step aside."

"I can't let you in."

"Ma'am, I could arrest you right now for obstruction of justice. Is that how you want this to go?"

"I can't let you in."

"You are getting very close to a world of pain."

"That's him right there."

She could hear Jamie's measured tones. She crouched still lower, waiting for the gunshot, but in the din of breath and blood she couldn't hear it. She clutched at her chest for the water filter that wasn't there. Her fingers scrabbled on the foreign surface of her T-shirt.

"Reka. Darling, you can get down."

Time had fled from her. She looked down at Aimee's raised and anxious face. From the front room Jamie said: "Well, this moves up our time frame."

She lay in bed shaking. Later, Zaiden came. "Is she okay? What happened?" she heard his sweet voice ask. "Oh Jesus," he said, closer now, "what did they do to her?"

"Excuse me, who are you?"

"I heard them but I didn't want to come out. I didn't want to make trouble for you."

Aimee pressed in. "Are you the Phelpses'—um, offspring?" she said. "Can you move away from the bed?"

"Go away," Reka rasped. They both leapt back. "You want us to go?" Aimee said.

"Aimee go away."

She yanked Zaiden down to the bed. He got under the covers and put his arms around her. She pressed up against his loose morning breasts, into the comforting scent of his shaving cream, as with cool lips he kissed her forehead and the sides of her eyes. "Poor bunny," he said, "poor little Reka-bun," and held her tight.

"Get the board president to sign it. I can't right now, there's something at home. Well, can you tap her? Maybe the treasurer. Hold on a sec, I'll check." She saw Reka. "I'll tap you right back."

She put down the tap-tap and said gravely, "I'm so sorry that happened. And I'm glad your friend was here to help."

"He's not an offspring," Reka said, and Aimee said, "I know. I apologize."

"Are they going to come back?" She hated the uncontrollable heartbeat that made the question shake in her mouth. How she wished she could be twenty, or however old Aimee was. Big enough to fight the polices at the door, as Aimee had not done. Big enough to shoot them dead.

"Sweetheart, I don't know."

Zaiden would go with her. He loathed his life here, he told her that every day. He could disguise himself as a police and get Reka over. They would find the people who had destroyed Reka's nest. They would join the Brothers ...

"How would you feel about that?"

"You mean adopting me?" Reka said.

"I mean, down the line, if that's something you would be comfortable with. But I'm thinking in terms of right now, we could sort of relocate? Like, imminently. Maybe to California. Or Hawaii. Hawaii might be good. You could go to school, I bet you'd like that. No lawyers, no lawsuits," Aimee said. "Just me and you."

Lore had said this would happen. Not that Reka was happy with Lore, who had done plenty of things she shouldn't have. Lore had abandoned her when she had dysentery and Lore had abandoned her in this house. And still the love of Lore was so violent inside her that she had to wrestle it down.

She'd said: "You should stay on this side. They'll iron out the logistics."

"I don't know what logistics means."

"Technicalities. Like your immigration status and whatever."

"What's my immigration status?"

"Well, we're all illegal. But he's a lawyer, they can fix that. You'd have plenty to eat, you know," Lore said. "You could grow properly. And Aimee is a good woman."

"I hate her."

"You'll get over it."

"I want to stay with you."

She had slept in Lore's arms as she did in Zaiden's, but Lore was her flesh and skin and hair. They were sister creatures, and she belonged with Lore. She offered to be

Lore's assistant. Like one of her ladies, and she explained what ladies were, which made Lore smile that upside-down smile. But Lore said she wasn't a queen. She was a person who had been stuck in some sharp places and broken, and she didn't work right anymore, and Reka could not come where a broken person would go.

When she knocked, Zaiden was ready. He came out carrying the ladder and a plastic shopping bag and wearing his backpack. They got the ladder into the elevator without being seen, because it was very late at night.

"I don't know if it will reach," he said. But Reka said she could climb. They carried it—Zaiden carried it—out into the parking lot, where a cool-edged breeze lifted Zaiden's hair. It was the first time Reka had been chilly since she got here, and only the second time she'd been out in the open. She thought again of Sterling Teacher, the grown-up who climbed walls like a spider, and wondered if Sterling was broken too.

The higher she went on the ladder, the more the breeze blew. She could feel the steps swaying under her feet, and she was very scared, especially when she got to the top of the ladder and had to stand on it to reach the first metal rung. She was sure she was going to fall backwards. She felt the world begin to tip, and terror and the determination to live both slammed into her at once. She reached for the rung and grabbed it. The next was around the curve of the billboard pole and seemed very far away. She got it and then she was dangling by her hands, one foot still hooked on the ladder, and she began to giggle in short, uncontrollable bursts. How could she pull herself up? She did it, with a terrific wrench to her arms. She put a foot on each rung and climbed, hugging the pole. It was almost as wide as she was. Her body was vibrating with fear and anticipation. She felt sure she was going to pee. She struggled through a hole in the platform. Now the metal slats were under her feet, and the plastic bag had twisted in the climb like a tourniquet around her shoulder. She fumbled it off and took out the spray paint.

Painting was harder than you might think. She and Zaiden had practiced on the walls of his room, writing "R+Z 4ever" and "Fuck You" in gold, but for the billboard Reka had insisted on red. Reka the Red, that was her. She aimed high. She had imagined the words covering the entire picture and blocking out the advertiser's slogan, but now saw she was going to have to place them close together near the bottom. Clumsily, she shot paint onto the board in the shape of a cross. Then parallel lines with a bar. Then a line up and down. Then one wavy line.

T   H I   S

Progress was so slow—

P I CTU RE W AS

—that she almost gave up. Her arms ached. But she was not leaving here without leaving her words.

Zaiden was miserable when she got down. In the light of other billboards she could see him cringing. "Come on, Zaiden!" she said, but he wouldn't go. He stammered and pushed his hair and she realized he was afraid of her. Afraid of Reka! A small sadness pierced her and was swiftly borne away on a flood of excitement and pride. She could hurt people now. For the very first time in her life she saw how powerful she was going to be.

"It's my parents," he said, and she didn't even care that he had two parents he loved, or that he preferred to scurry home to his plaid shirts and warm quilts instead of staying with her. "We don't want people like you anyway," she said. She didn't care one bit. She could hardly feel the spurt of pain as she crushed the tenderness between them, at all.

At the end of the parking lot she looked back. Zaiden was still standing under the billboard, but she didn't see him, only the magnificent red scrawl.

THIS PICTURE WAS STOLEN FROM ME
AS I SHALL STEAL YOUR SLEEP   REKA

"Whether you go into it willingly or not, asleep or awake, there will be a reckoning."

Amazing that she could say those words to him while chained to the floor. Was she delusional? Did she believe herself the next leader of the blacks? But he knew what answer she would make almost before she made it. "I'm just a conduit for the voice speaking through me."

"The voice of God?" he said, openly smirking.

"Some would say."

"And what do you say?"

"I call it the voice of love, Eddie. The love that can reunite you with yourself."

The body that birthed him was a black woman's. He knew that much, though not her name or where she was now. He was born well before Partition, so she'd probably lived right there in Cedar Rapids with the rest of them. The Eddys were wealthy; his father was a state senator, his mother a philanthropist. He was called William after his father, and Cleveland was a family name, given, he presumed, to further cement him into whiteness, though it was also a black man's name and thus betrayed, like everything they did, the niggling doubt at the bottom of the treasures they heaped upon him.

They told him eventually—he supposed because he was a difficult child and somebody had advised them that it might help. His father gave him the facts and left the sincerity to his mother. "We are your family of choice. We specifically chose you because we loved you so much." A vapid sentiment, even to a ten-year-old. "This is something we keep private, Willie, do you understand?" What he understood was that everything was private. He had no reason to make a full and accurate accounting of himself to anyone, and many reasons not to—a lesson he had also learned from watching his father in public life. As he grew older, he found it easiest to have no system of accounts at all. Feelings didn't stay with him, nor did attachments. What flowed in and out of his secret self was no more real than what he represented to the world. He was a man without a core.

What he'd told Sterling was true, although that gave it no more value in his mind than the statements he'd made which were false. He had tried a lot of things before coming to the B.B.P. At nineteen he was in drug rehab in Alaska, at twenty-three he was teaching prep school and sleeping with his students. He dabbled in busking, merchandising, investments, copywriting, modeling, and tapnet fraud. He taught English in Hungary and administered microcredit in India during the Sirocco-Vesperian war. Then he came home and tapped the recruiter who had contacted him in college. He had, at present, a girlfriend named Amanda and a very pleasant apartment downtown, and he had found in the Bureau an adequate staging ground for his intellectual restlessness and his craving for conquest.

He was also telling the truth when he said he liked her. The majority of his work was punishingly boring, and Sterling had provided him with six years of extracurricular interest. More, she was the occasion of his final triumph over a superior he despised, a bureaucrat named Doug, and she was a woman, which always made things lively. His staff had proven their loyalty by running the data after hours, in defiance of Doug: every name of every resident within six miles of the popshow district, cross-referenced with buying records from the past twenty years. The names that didn't match up were people without chips—about three hundred of them—and two of his best girls worked through the list, observing, tailing and even interviewing, eliminating prospect after prospect as too timid, too dumb or too fat. A couple of years in, they came across Sterling. The instant he set eyes on her, he knew. In that spartan office with two of the walls disabled, head down and growling at all comers, she had "sociopath" written all over her like the very brands she cut out of her clothes.

North Harbor was not SAPID, however, and the word of William Eddy was not sufficient to send a woman to prison for an indefinite period of time. His people had swept every culvert and parking lot in a ten-mile radius, using both metal detection and sonar, without finding her cache. People higher than Doug were watching him, and quarterly budget-to-actuals were coming out. He needed a bone. So he went to Lore.

It was not easy getting in to see her, either procedurally or physically. She was being held deep inside the wall, in a place Cleveland had never been (previously, on his way to SAPID, he'd crossed in an armored car). The wall was in a blighted part of town, though perhaps it had been less blighted before the wall—he wouldn't know. He did know that an effort had been made to isolate existing black populations on the far side of the barrier, which was why it took such an intricately winding path across the state, and why it crossed only a narrow portion of North Harbor. Apart from old factories and warehouses, and the empty roads running directly into the wall, the land here was given over to weeds. The wall itself was vast, half as high as a skyscraper and extending to the limit of visibility in both directions. Here and there it had assimilated a derelict building, half-choking the old structure with cement so that just a turret or a patch of brick surfaced in its uniform pour. Other than those, the only feature of the massive concrete panels were the seeping stains of darkness, like shadow drapery, left by the falling rain.

Her cell was several miles away from the point where he entered the wall, a distance he traveled by golf cart, chatting with two soldiers. They took him up in an elevator and walked him down a long hallway lined with narrow doors. Above the handle on each door was printed a number— 2.135, 2.136, and so on. They stopped at 2.148 and let him in, closing the door behind him. "Alone at last," he said.

She sat on a concrete bench molded into the concrete

wall. Her wrists and ankles were in cuffs attached by lengths of heavy chain to a bolt in the middle of the floor. She smiled when she saw him but said nothing. "May I?" he said, and she slid over to give him a seat.

"I notice that whenever we get a chance for a little tête-à-tête, you're locked up somewhere."

"Maybe that's because you don't think of us as equals," she answered. She sounded slightly hoarse, as if coming down with a cold.

"On the contrary, as I've explained. I don't think of us as equals because you're always locked up."

"A sad failure of imagination on your part."

"Tell me about Teacher."

"What's to know?" Lore said. "She's lonely."

"About her method. Her strategy. How does she pick her targets?"

"She's dying to talk about it. All you have to do is ask."

"I don't think I have quite the same effect on her as a cute black girl from the ghetto."

"If I had known the point was picking up girls, I would have been over here a long time ago," Lore said. There was a sore on her mouth. With both hands she pulled one leg over the other, making the chains clank. "Are you hurt?" he asked, out of curiosity.

"Just stiff."

"Are they torturing you or something?" Even to him, that sounded uncivil. "I mean," he amended, "do they do that sort of thing here?"

"Usually torture is conducted in a dedicated facility," the prisoner said. "If you put torturers in too much of an open environment, they might not do it."

"Only might?" He was aware that the conversation was getting away from him but didn't mind.

"It's very easy to get one human being to brutalize another," Lore said. "All you have to do is separate them from themselves. You would be the perfect torturer."

"I feel I'm a nicely integrated person, actually."

That was when she told him that he could not escape his race. He said she obviously didn't know him very well.

"I'm not talking about people finding out. Though we are being recorded."

He glanced up at the camera. "Recordings can be erased."

"Of course. But trying to erase your truth, that's what does the real damage. You're carving yourself up, Eddie. Every day you're less and less of a man."

"Let me ask you something," he said. "Where does this truth reside? It can't be detected in a blood test or an x-ray. It's not in my DNA." He had made sure of all this early in his career. "It's not visible to the naked eye."

"Not to the white eye."

"Whatever. It doesn't affect my earning power, it doesn't limit my housing choices, it has no influence on my life at all. So where is it?"

"Are you happy?"

"Very."

"Are you?"

He became aware that she smelled stale, with a hint of urine. Sighing, he put away the tap-tap he'd been holding at the ready. "I wish you a good afternoon," he said.

Lore pulled up a hand to scratch behind her ear. "So you're trying to put her in jail?" she asked.

"I am putting her in jail."

"But you need information."

"That would speed things up."

"I'll help you," she said, "if you do something for me."

"What?"

"Get a message to her."

He said promptly, for the camera, "Anything you tell me, I have an obligation to disclose."

"I need to write it down."

Getting a sheet of paper and a writing implement took a long time. He did nothing himself, but waited as his requisition was tapped all over the structure and a cadet finally came running up, breathless, with the materials in a sealed pouch. He could get used to this, William Eddy thought. The comfort of command. He took the pouch in to Lore, who was curled tightly on the concrete bench, apparently sleeping, the four chains trailing from her like the moorings of a ship.

"Will this do?"

She hauled herself up, laid the paper on the bench and began carefully scripting letters. He watched the top of her bent head, which was shaved down to the skin. He could see an old nick in the scalp that was almost white. Her clothes were filthy, and he wondered what she would look like as a normal person, with hair. It was hard to imagine. At last she handed him the letter. He read it and stood up.

"Make sure she understands," Lore said.

William Eddy nodded. Folding the paper neatly, he went to the door. As it opened he glanced back and saw her sitting as she had been when he entered, hands in her lap. He paused.

"What does it feel like to know you're going to die?"

Lore looked at him seriously. She said, "What does it feel like for you?"

Prison, like any closed system, could be cracked. She could probably crack it in about ten years. But she didn't want to spend ten years shoveling herself out of the shit Lore had dropped her into, and there was also the popshow to consider. She could barely stand to be outside anymore, let alone in a small locked room where popshow played continuously over every surface. She had a suspicion that ten years of that exposure would actually drive her mad.

Her mind worked and worked without effect. It was like a tap-tap looking for a signal. And inside and outside its oscillations was Lore.

Aimee was in a state: she looked like she had been robbed in the street. "She's gone. Reka!" she said when Sterling asked who. "She ran away. Or maybe they found her." She went into the bathroom, came out with a wad of toilet paper and blew her nose. "Oh, God, Sterling, she could be anywhere."

"At least she's not with you."

"What?"

"You can't be arrested for possession of stolen property."

"Oh, God," Aimee said again. She pressed the tissue all over her face. "Why did I come to you?"

"I don't know," Sterling said. "I have a lot to do."

"I woke up this morning and she was gone. The only thing she took was that filter thingy she wears around her neck. She didn't take food or clothes or anything! And she wrote—" She lowered her voice. "I think she wrote on the jumbo outside."

"I'm pretty busy right now."

She was kneading the tissue into wet pulp in her hands. "I asked her to go away with me. This court case and every-thing, it's not going to work … She didn't give it a thought. She'd rather be out there, with the people who want to grab her and lock her up and exploit her, than with me." Her voice cracked. "He can't get any information. He tried all week, he asked prosecutors, judges, he talked to people in the military—no one will say anything. She could be dead."

"You said she just left."

"She was standing right there and I didn't help her. I just let it happen."

Sterling realized the antecedent had changed. "They had guns," she suggested. Aimee squeezed her eyes shut, but tears crept into her lashes. "All my life I've been thinking about what I would do in a situation like that," she said. "How I would stand up. How I would interrupt injustice, if I were ever lucky enough to see it happening right in front of my eyes."

"There was nothing you could have done."

"How can you say that, Sterling? If that had been a—a jumbo someone was putting up, you would have done something. You would have smashed it to pieces."

"Not with the police there. Not in a room full of people."

She kept trying to enunciate as her voice wobbled wildly. "I thought I was a real person, you know? The right kind of person. That's all that's gotten me through. I'm fat, I'm emotional, I'm not very smart but I'm trying to do some-thing to change the world. You know I have a B.B.P. file, right? They have a file on me. So I must be a good person, right? But it turns out I'm just like every other little piggy slurping up popshow on this side of the w-wall." She gave in and started to sob. "Please, Sterling, please help me. I can't bear this. I don't know what to do."

It shocked her to be solicited so desperately. She couldn't remember the last time it had happened—the last time someone besides Lore had come to her assuming she had something to give. All she knew how to do was take things away.

"How can I help you? I don't even know what you're crying about," she said.

Aimee hid her face in tissue-flecked hands and wept. "Okay, okay," Sterling said. Every minute she sat mewling there was another minute Sterling was not solving the problem of her future. "Aimee, listen."

Her old lover, inflamed mouth trembling, stopped crying and tried to meet her eyes. When they had first known each other, Sterling had thought Aimee might be the end of pain. She was kind and good, she was beautiful, and she listened to the history of Sterling's suffering and believed. Then came I.U., and the university funding it had accepted, and Sterling was alone again, and the drilling of the world into her was worse because she had dreamed of its removal. She remembered trusting Aimee just that much. She said to her now, "The problem is not you. The problem is outside of you. You have to remember that."

"If I were a real person, it would be me going over instead of you."

"What?" Sterling said.

"It would be me going over instead of you."

"No, why did you say that? Who told you I'm going over?"

Aimee looked at her in surprise, her nose dripping mucus. "Lore did."

On her way out she met someone in the hallway who greeted her by name. Aimee's still-raw voice echoed back, vaguely puzzled: "Do I know you from ... Are you with the New Harbor Foundation?"

"Oh, I work with Sterling," Cleveland said.

He came in, frowning. "It's beyond inconvenient that you don't have a tap-tap."

"Why don't you buy me one?"

"Because you'd bury it in a sewer pipe and I'd be out the expense." He looked around the apartment, smoothing the front of his Digby Duplessis shirt. "Are you Wrecka?"

"What?"

"Are you Wrecka, R-E-K-A, however it's pronounced?"

"I don't know what you're talking about."

"Beyond inconvenient," Cleveland said. "It's like we have no common ground at all."

He tapped something up and showed it to her. She looked at Reka's handiwork for a second, thinking, Not bad for fifty-one inches tall and under seventy pounds.

"I need to know if you had anything to do with this."

"Why do you ask?"

"Give me a straight fucking answer, please. This is business."

"No," Sterling said. "That wasn't me."

"Thank you." He put the tap-tap away. "We need to talk."

He said Sterling's arraignment was set for the morning. What was she being arraigned on? The expected. "You know, violence against corporate bodies, subversive activity, defamation, reduction of brand value, interfering with the flow of commerce." Fifteen to life, he was thinking.

"And what's your evidence," she said, "the letter of recommendation?"

"It would've been enough to get us rolling."

But things had changed. When the language went up on the No Name jumbo, all hell broke loose. "I had people from Counterintelligence tapping me at three in the morning, asking what I knew about Wrecka. Asking if you could give information. Or if it was you. Somebody's face is red, I think. Somebody had a clever idea, it backfired, and now they want to contain it before the public starts asking questions."

"Questions?" she said.

" 'Why do black people hate us?'—that kind of thing. And coupled with your friend's little speech," Cleveland said. "There's no telling what kind of bullshit could bubble up. Then you're looking at a major community pacification initiative by Sirocco, not to mention finding the kid and eliminating her, which is not cheap. You know, with equipment, training, counseling and what have you, killing is probably the most expensive thing that we do." He thought Sterling was staring at him, though she was actually calculating what advantage she could gain from this situation. So far she had come up with a null set. "It's usually referred to as population adjustment, but I say why not call a spade a spade?" This seemed to strike him as humorous, and he laughed shortly before returning to the subject. "They're going to fuck up my case. I know they are."

"You mean my case."

"They're going to lay this thing on you and muddy up my fucking case."

"That must be painful for you." She had planned this, all of it. She had written Sterling's ending like a book.

He took out his tap-tap, checked his tie, checked his hair, opened the device and took out a mint, closed it and put it back in his pocket. "There are things you don't know about me."

"So you've said."

"Would you like a SacréMint?" He seemed not to notice that he had just popped it in his mouth. "Very refreshing. Do you have any ideas?"

"Ideas?" Sterling said. None of her own.

He listened carefully. "And I gain precisely what?"

"Not losing me to those assholes. You're in control."

Head bowed, he was deep in himself, thinking. "What if I were to give you an hour?"

"Sorry?"

"I could do it tonight. Say at midnight. Make it look like a scheduling error."

She said nothing. The biggest job of her life, the most secure barricade in the world, no prep time, no recon, no pen testing, and he wanted to give her an hour? He was Mother Teresa. "Take it," he said, "it's all I can do."

She sat motionless in the dark, waiting for her night vision to return. She could feel her heart beating. For the first time in what seemed like months she remembered her truth: all accomplishment was solitary. With other people came confusion, distortion, forgetting, distraction.

"They mentioned a piano factory. I don't know where

it is, but apparently it's the fastest way to get to your ciga-rettes if you left them on the other side. They really care about their cigarettes."

"They just happened to mention that? The best way to get across?"

"I asked them," he'd said. "Perhaps you've noticed that if you ask people something they give you the answer. It's a principle of social engineering."

"What do you know about social engineering?"

"I do it for a living."

That was the only information he had. "One hour," he reminded her as he left. It would take thirty minutes just to get across town. But when you have no choice, she understood, you have no doubts. She put it all aside as she sat there—everything holding her to this life, which she lifted from herself and removed like a suit of clothes, and the small, writhing pulp of her emotions, and Lore.

Schoolgirl | Day 25

A couple of tires, a mattress blackened by bedbugs, an iron pipe, a dead tree sticking up in the middle of a pile of rubble. She crawled into the pipe. It jutted out of the rubble towards the city, facing away from the polices patrolling the wall, and she pulled a tire over the opening and slept like a baby for the rest of the night.

She had debated with herself about the ladies. She missed them. But were they really what she needed right now? Maybe they kept her too much company. Maybe if she hadn't been corseted ... cosseted by their attentions, she would have been more alert when Edmark and Owen came to take her. Besides, the ladies were sure to be frightened by this situation. They wouldn't know what to make of it, and they would wander lost, with their reticules and dimity, among the rocks. Reka didn't have time for that.

The burning heat of the pipe's corrugations stung her awake. Sunlight glared through the middle of the tire and the air was unbreathably thick. She moved the tire, panting, and cautiously stuck her head out. No men were visible on the expanse of weedy road before her, but an army truck went by, rocketing over broken concrete and scattering chunks of brick. She pulled her head back in. She began to feel hungry, and she wasn't used to being hungry anymore. It was awful. She thought of Aimee's maple cream and almost decided to go back. But she was a black woman, and black women belonged with black men fighting for freedom. When night came she would find a way across.

She eased out of the pipe. Crouched at its mouth, she raised her head until she could look across its curved back towards the wall. The wall was gigantic, taller than any building Reka had ever seen, colored a dull yellow-gray. It was not a wall you could stick things in, like her pitty wall back home. It wasn't holding up a bridge. It was only there to be colossal and hateful. If you got together all the Brothers on the other side of the wall, and all the Kidlanders and some of those other people who just walked around scaring everyone, she bet you could break through it. Kill some guards and find their secret tunnels or even climb right over it. Maybe her people hadn't thought about this or maybe they were considering it even now, but Reka would call them to action, Reka the Red. Not in make-believe but, she knew with sudden certainty, in real life. The knowledge of her destiny filled her with happiness and peace.

There was an abandoned housing project across the road, its rows of windows just square holes without glass. She looked back at the wall. The day was gray but clear, and she would be visible from all sides as she crossed the road. She inched out, peeked both ways, and ran. She reached up to the nearest windowsill, jumping to get her hands on it, and heaved herself up; every muscle above her waist tore, worse than the time on the billboard pole, and then she was over. She fell into dust and dirt. Her water filter had swung behind her and now stabbed her in the small of the back. She hugged her legs tightly and rolled over onto her side, repeating in a new hard tone, "Don't cry, don't cry."

Thirteen and a half hours later, Sterling walked by the old projects. Unlike Reka, she didn't crouch or run. She was dressed in dark blue clothes and a blue cap and carried only three small picks. She felt amazingly light. When Reka called to her she kept walking for a few steps, then came back and looked into the empty window frame. She saw a pigtailed head bobbing up and down. "You came," the child whispered.

"Don't whisper. It carries."

"Are you going over?"

"You need to go home."

Having gathered momentum, she scrambled onto the sill. "Let's go, Sterling, let's go right now."

"Go back to Aimee," Sterling said. Her chances of survival were sinking by the second. She looked around at the still-silent road. Reka's weight struck her shoulders, and the hoarse voice said, "Take me." She even kicked at the wall, as if Sterling were a boat she could push off. Sterling felt herself begin to topple. She staggered backwards and put both arms around Reka, and as the little body clung to her they became, for an instant, that single animal once more. "Jesus," Sterling murmured. She shifted Reka onto her back.

"How are we going?"

"Just be quiet."

Any plan would be completely fucked up by now, so it was just as well she had none. She walked across the shattered road and up to the wall. They were close enough to touch its gritty surface. Reka reached out to do so and Sterling took her wrist and pulled it back in, feeling the small hand under her hand. They moved northward along the wall until Sterling saw lights. A section ahead of them was brightly floodlit, with soldiers bivouacked in trailers among jeeps and portable toilets; against the curve of the wall it looked almost a mile long. She bent to one side and let Reka off. Then she gripped her firmly by the upper arm and marched her into the light.

There was an insectile rush of weaponry being cocked. "B.B.P.!" Sterling said.

"Hands up!"

"If I let go she'll run."

A soldier came up, edging sideways as if Reka were a bomb, and grabbed her away from Sterling. Holding the kid away from him with one arm and pointing his gun at Sterling with the other, he said, "Hands up." She said, "Joint Task Force on Subversion. Don't you tap the news?"

"I don't care if it's the Joint Task Force on Anal Sex, get your hands up."

She did. "Take a look at what you've got there."

Reka was trying to pull free of the soldier. He called another, who hiked her into the air and held her against his chest while she struggled. "Hey, it's No Name Jeans," said a soldier behind the first one. Reka writhed more violently. "I hate you!" she screamed at Sterling. The man holding her asked, "Did she really write that message?"

"No, that was part of the campaign," said another.

"I heard there's really no such thing as No Name Jeans," said a third.

"Bullshit. I know somebody who bought them."

"They don't have them here."

"It was in Kenosha."

"Why would someone in fucking Kenosha be able to buy No Name Jeans when we don't have them here?"

"Test market," another soldier opined. The first one said, "Jesus Christ, shut up." He adjusted his mark on Sterling. "Tell me what you're doing here."

"I'm taking her through the piano factory."

"Why the fuck are you doing that?"

"She's bait. I have a target on the other side."

This soldier looked capable of thought. He was young, and she could see a Lollytat on his hand. "I need ID," he said.

"I don't have any."

"You fucking barge into my camp at midnight with the pickaninny off the No Name flats and you don't have any fucking ID?"

"I'm undercover, Captain Brant," said Sterling, observing the tag over his sewn-on sponsorship logo (One Pill Lifts Depression For Thirty-Three Hours: ALYTHEA). "I haven't used my real name in fifteen years."

"Murph, tap Executive," he said, raising his voice. She raised hers: "Executive doesn't know about me. Are you going to let me through? Or are you going to risk that my contact at the other end panics and does something we're all going to regret?"

"What about her?" He tilted his head at screeching Reka, who was kicking the soldier who held her with such force that he was almost dancing. "You're going to take that across by yourself?"

She walked up to the second soldier, followed by the gun sight of the first, and hit Reka in the face. She had never hit a person before, but it didn't hurt too much. Reka's head jerked back and thumped her guardian, who was so surprised he lost his grip and had to catch her by the armpits just before she slid to the ground.

"Now get us to the piano factory," Sterling said.

The floor was very old and had been through a lot. It had a beautiful coat of varnish on it, as if glaze could make up for the deep gouges, the scars, the abrasions, the plugs of metal. Sterling said, "It's faster if I carry you."

She had tried to run away through the corridors, but Sterling caught up to her easily and did carry her, then, until Reka squirmed down and followed sullenly behind. She understood that she was alone and very short and that all she had in the world, apart from her dreams of how things would be, was this adult who had assaulted her and perhaps broken an important bone in her face. Yet she still wanted to put her head down on Sterling's shoulder and ride in her arms. You must not, she told herself. You must not love.

They turned and went past two huge doors, bolted together like Frankenstein and painted dark brown, with a pulley system on them that was also painted brown. If Hell was an endless dungeon with vaulted ceilings and dead-end walls of stone, plus white doors and corridors that had been stuck inside it to give people places to live but the people were all gone, these would be the gates of Hell. She shivered in the cold. They were going down a cement stair, very clammy, with horrible gray tendrils of dust on every step, and then Sterling stopped, opened a door with her picky sticks and looked out. Reka, peeking behind her, saw a small courtyard surrounded by brick walls. Against the walls were several large pots holding the crumbling remains of plants, and in the middle of the yard was a dead cat. "Shit," Sterling said. She closed the door. Very clearly they both heard, in a man's voice, the words "distribution report."

"I'll get you your distribution report," said a second, younger voice. It came from the top of the stairs.

"In file exchange format?"

"You want your shit moved or not?"

"Of course we want it moved, that's what you're doing here," the first said. He sounded like police. "But if you can't follow protocol, there are plenty of other actors who can move it for us."

"Think it a goddamn theater class or something," the younger one muttered. The police voice said, "Just make sure you report within six weeks."

"Look, this is Kidlander efficiency. Your shit be gone in a day and a half."

"Really? That's two hundred kilos."

"It better be."

Reka began crawling up the stairs. She felt Sterling's hand on her ankle and kicked. A tap-tap beeped, and the soldier said, "I'm going to have to leave you here."

"What about our safe conduct?"

"You'll get it outside. We have a situation in the east wing." Boots struck the floor, and Reka stuck her head up over the stairwell. She saw a number of boys, Kidlanders, with a number of duffel bags, and in their center a boy with a sparse beard and a gold ring in his nose. "Royal!" she hissed as loudly as she dared, and when he whipped around with his knife she tried very hard not to pee.

He said he would take her but he couldn't do nothing for Sterling. "Why you running around with a white lady anyway? In the middle of their whole military-industrial complex? Shit, schoolgirl, you got a death wish."

"She's my friend," Reka said, but her fingers crept up to her face. Royal glanced down the stairs at Sterling, who was standing there waiting. He had warned her not to come any closer. "I tell you for free, that ain't no friend," he said. "Polka."

"Yes, Cap."

"Give me your hat."

"Aw, Cap."

"Give me your hat, motherfucker, or I'll cut you like a bitch." He started fitting it over Reka's hair. "You think you droll, but it not so fucking droll when I lose my patience," he said. His fingers were hard, knocking on her skull as he jerked the hat down to her eyes. "You hear me?"

"Yes, Cap."

"Give her a duffel."

She staggered under the weight. "Okay, you a dog now," Royal said. "Let's go."

Cap and dogs moved out, marching through the maze of corridors. Royal kept Reka in front of him, nudging her right or left, and sometimes she felt the pull on her shoulders ease for a minute as her duffel was lifted into the air. They descended a steep, winding metal staircase; the boys behind Reka seemed to press forward, whether with anxiety or gravity, as if they were about to tumble down on top of her. The floor was rough underfoot, and the smell was awful. When Royal's flashlight jumped, the walls showed furry with grime and webs of dust, and shadows lolled over broken furniture. They turned and went through a passage small enough that only Reka could walk upright, and she flinched so violently against the broken stones that Royal had to put the head of the flashlight in her back and push. She could feel the neat circle it made on her spine and thought of the disc of light trapped there, leaping out into brightness and then instantly thinning to nothing as he moved the flashlight away. They entered a room with low wooden rafters and a cement wall that bulged inward at the bottom, as if its matter had settled over many years, and shouldered their way through smaller free-standing walls that were lined up like an obstacle course. Reka's duffle banged into one of the walls, which gave out a clangorous moan. She was nearly brought up short with the understanding that they were all pianos standing on end.

"No dreaming, schoolgirl."

"Can I stay with you?"

He didn't answer. She asked again when they were in the jostling truck, getting their S.C. past the soldiers. Some of the other dogs heard and looked from her to Royal with keen attention. She explained her idea. Royal said, "We can't be invading the people we doing business with."

"But then you'd be the ruler. You wouldn't have to sell gem."

"Girl, you don't understand economics."

"Just let me stay," she said. "I'll be the best dog. Better than these guys."

For some reason they all laughed. Royal was frowning and staring straight ahead. She noticed the neat way his beard was trimmed and a puckered scar on his cheek. The scar looked like someone had taken a needle, caught the underside of his skin and pulled. "You need to shut the fuck up," he said. "This is no place for you."

Day 1

The air is no fresher on this side of the wall, but no fouler, either. There are no jumbos on the deserted road, no hypes on the crumbling walls, nowhere the intimation of a single brand. She is alone in a landscape of complete silence. It is what she has fought for all her life, and it feels unreal, frictionless, as if she isn't really here at all.

Along the road are some crooked structures that were once townhouses, each standing in an empty lot with the ghosts of its neighbors imprinted on its sides. She needs to get farther away from the wall. The people inside made clear to her that, without qualification and ID, she can be picked up again at any time. "So get your business done," said the head interrogator, who viewed her with open disgust after keeping her awake for forty-eight hours without results, "and try to come back, God help you."

Her footsteps crunch the gravel. Scattered between the houses are sprung sofas, tufted with stuffing and sodden from weather, and a few of the old-style televisions of her childhood with their screens smashed in. After about two miles the road ends, so she steps off into the tall weeds and strikes west. There are people here, hauling bags and luggage trolleys through the broken stalks. When she tries speaking to them they ignore her. Finally someone stops: a man in his fifties, wearing a Pink Devils War On Breast Cancer baseball hat—the first piece of branded clothing she's seen since coming out of the wall—and a cheerful demeanor. "Where you want to go?" he says.

"Freesia Street."

"Well, damn, I don't think I should tell you—you look like some kind of police spy or something."

"I'm not a spy," she says. "If they wanted to spy on you, they would send black people."

"Ain't that the truth," says the man. He takes off his hat and smoothes sweat from his bald head. It is midday and hot. "You know them folks on Freesia Street?"

"I know one. Lore."

"Never met the lady," he says. "And what's your honorable name?" His is Ronald. "I tell you what, Sterling, because you seem like a straight shooter, and I like straight shooters. All this stuff about color, I can't get behind it, you know? We all one race. Just as long as I don't take a drink and the good Lord's watching over me, I'm satisfied," Ronald says. He has a cart hidden down there by the willow tree. If she pushes it for him, he'll take her to Freesia Street.

It turns out to be a large shopping cart laden with every type of junk, from books to dishes to tennis rackets, which is nearly impossible to propel from clod to clod of weed-choked earth. She labors, sweating, while Ronald talks about his daughters, his sobriety, and his girlfriend Donna. When she hits a rock and overturns the whole load, she says, "Your system is fucked."

"What's that?"

"This vehicle is incompatible with the terrain. You should get a motorbike and a trailer."

"Now, that's an idea. I will definitely consider that," Ronald says.

He shares his lunch, one shrunken apple and a slice of bread so stale it's hard to chew. Sterling can't wait to get to the people who know what they're about. With time and a base of operations, she can infiltrate the wall for them; analyze Sirocco's organization, work out a plan of attack. Her empty stomach vies in hunger with her fighting heart.

They arrive at dusk, and Ronald tells her to wait at the bottom of the hill. "Why?" she says.

"I wouldn't want the good people of Freesia Street to start associating my high-quality merchandise with someone of your persuasion."

"I thought you didn't believe in color."

"What I believe I believe, but this is business," Ronald says. She watches him trundling his cart slowly up the street. All around her are trees, which surprises her because she thought SAPID was a wasteland. The trees are full of birds. Their shrill argument rises into the lavender sky, and then the birds themselves rise, wheel across its fading face, bank in formation, choose another tree and resume their caucus.

A man is descending the street towards her. His fluffy pewter-colored hair and long beard make his head seem too ponderous for his body, which is clothed in thin trousers and a suit jacket. On his feet are leather sandals. He offers a dainty, long-nailed hand. "I understand you have a message for me," he says.

She hands him the letter, which the men in the wall allowed her to keep. He holds it up to the last light to read it. As he reads he scratches his chin through the beard, and once he smiles.

"Where is she now?" he asks. She says she doesn't know. Ira finishes scratching his chin. "She's in your city?" he says. "She chose to stay?"

"She was arrested."

Three people have come up behind him: a girl in tight jeans and a tight shirt with her hair in thick beaded braids, an old woman who walks with a cane, and a child. "Hi, Sterling," the child says. "Hi," says Sterling. The woman and the girl read the letter, frowning. "She say she in jail?" the old lady says.

"I need a place to sleep and some food," Sterling says.

Ira says, "We appreciate your coming all this way to deliver this message."

"I'm ready to work. That letter says I can work."

"She can climb walls," Reka says. "She rescued me from that place."

"She give you a fat lip," the girl says. She pulls Reka to her, and the child's arms embrace her solid hips. "You stay away from her."

"Did you work to keep her out of jail?" Ira asks Sterling. Something—bafflement, chagrin, ten hours of pushing a grocery cart in the hot sun—makes her raise her voice and say, "She walked into jail! There was nothing anybody could do."

"Real talk," says Reka's friend. "Can't say a word to her when she fixing to do something stupid."

"Do you have any way to communicate with her?" Ira says.

"Are you or are you not aware of my situation?" says Sterling. "Are you aware that I can't go back?"

"We appreciate that," he says again. He turns and looks at the old woman. She comes closer on her cane—she is heavy, twice as big as her husband, and her face is gray under the eyes. "You must understand," she says, "we are not an army you can sign up for."

"I don't need to be in an army. I just need to work."

"Oh, we got work. We got empty houses to clean out. We got trash that needs burning. We got a food garden to restore."

"What Alice is saying, if I can speak for her"—he stops to check, and the old lady says, "You may."

"Is you can live here and work for your keep," Ira goes on. "We can put you in forty-eight, next to Reka and Deedee, and they can show you some of what needs to be done. But we have no mission to send you on."

"I didn't come to do housework."

"What you came for is not our responsibility," he says. "We're not your friends."

She thinks of going on her way, of fighting by herself in this silent land. But fighting what? She has no purpose now. Her skills are useless. Her history has been erased. She left nothing behind. She's hungry. She looks at Reka. "Forty-eight?" she says.

"She's in."

She smiled.

"That's it, you know. I can't keep track of her now."

"I won't need any more updates," said Lore. Her voice was small and throaty in the cell. "Oh," he said, "right." Last night, ridiculously, he hadn't slept. His eyeballs felt parched. He kept running over today's to-do list—doctor Teacher's file, contact a lawyer, catch up on tapmail, meet with his team.

He went on: "I got her over, actually. It was me."

She said nothing. She didn't talk much anymore. "She told them some fucking spy story, and they tapped me," he said. "And I said it was true."

"I'm proud of you," she said.

"Why?"

"You did something."

"I didn't do it for—" He wasn't sure. "I didn't do it for you," he said, "I don't think."

"Actions are what matter," Lore said.

Handled correctly, this little adventure need not impede his rise to department head. He surprised himself by saying, "I feel I want to make a change."

She always looked right at him when he spoke. She had narrow eyes, with whites like bloodied milk, which seemed clear because they were part of her clear, unguarded face. Her chin stuck out a little proud of her head. When she smiled her mouth went down, revealing two missing teeth, and her chin stuck out even more, and the eyebrows went up on her still-smooth forehead. How old was she, twenty-three? He thought about her when he was in bed with Amanda. Amanda's ivory limbs, his lovely bed.

"I want to change my life."

"That's easy to do."

"To really change ... it seems impossible." He would like

more time to talk to her. He had taken to coming every morning before work, and he'd gotten them to turn off the camera. Not that he'd said anything too revealing. A little about his chilly childhood in Cedar Rapids, and the move to a marble-floored mansion in Des Moines. Sometimes he came in and described a vase or chaise he'd purchased for the apartment. He'd told her how much he spent on cocaine. "To make things different from how they are. That doesn't seem like a realistic task."

It was strange, surpassingly strange, that she wouldn't be here tomorrow. Again he felt the unease that had displaced his sleep. He wanted to stay until the last moment, curled at her feet. That was enough to make him stand up and, standing, to wonder how you took leave of somebody with no future. What did you wish them? Another oddity was that he'd forgotten, until Lore said it, the word "goodbye." She said, "Take care of yourself, Eddie." He bent and kissed her shrunken hand.

By the time he pulled in at the office, he was calm enough to go inside. He stepped out of the car and looked up, noticing how bright and cloudless the sky was. The trees around the parking lot lifted their green crowns towards its pinnacle of blue, and the air smelled of blossom and coffee. It was a beautiful summer day.

Her executioner was not healthy. His skin was clay-colored, his huge sloping stomach was visible even under the armored vest, and his fingers were misshapen and puffy on the smooth black butt of his pistol. He pointed it at her, and she felt a rush of hot piss down her leg.

"Are you ready?" he said. She didn't answer. The pain burst through her like a shooting star. Then it was over, and she was so grateful for having lived.

Thank you to the friends who lent their help and expertise (all mistakes are mine): Ken Craggs on rock climbing, Camile O'Briant on photo shoots, Stephen Brophy on food co-ops, and Stefanie Grindle on legal strategy. The idea of the pricey popshow-free space came from Michael Beattie. Useful texts included Colman McCarthy's nonviolence curriculum and Ozymandias's sabotage handbook, both available online; *The Revolution Misses You* by Zack Exley; *The Shock Doctrine* and *No Logo* by Naomi Klein; *Ecodefense*, edited by Dave Foreman and Bill Haywood; *Ragnar's Urban Survival* by Ragnar Benson; George Lakey's "Strategizing for a Living Revolution" in *Globalize Liberation*, edited by David Solnit (thank you to the volunteer clerk at Lucy Parsons Bookstore who pointed me towards this book); *The True Confessions of an Albino Terrorist* by Breyten Breytenbach; *Kaffir Boy* by Mark Mathabane; *I, Rigoberta Menchú* by Rigoberta Menchú and Elisabeth Burgos-Debray; *Too Scared to Cry* by Lenore Terr. I also consulted the "torture memos" of the U.S. government.

Warm thanks go to Joanne McKenna and Jessica Sorkin and their families, and to Johnette Ellis; to Howard Jacobowitz and his (and my) family; to Carol Goldsmith Heines and Sandra Brant; to Christopher Vyce of the Brattle Agency for advice and support; to Devynity and, once again, Johnette for the cover; and to Eben Sorkin and Steve Wolf for allowing me to benefit from their talents.

Without the love and devotion of Kyle Katz I would be a smaller, colder person who probably could not have written this book.

Finally, I owe more than I can say to Letta Neely.